Liz

MW01515349

Welcome to New York :)

CALEM

NEW YORK CITY'S FINEST - BOOK ONE

CHRISTOPHER HARLAN

03.18

Liz

Welcome to New York!

Calem

New York's Finest Book 1

By Christopher Harlan

Cover design and **Formatting** by Jessica Hildreth
Proofreading by Marla at Proofing with Style

Warning:

Content contains explicit sexual content and adult content. It is intended for mature, adult audiences. Parental/reader discretion is advised.

DEDICATION

To my beautiful family – for always believing in me.

To my readers – welcome to New York, you're going to love it here. . .

AUTHOR'S NOTE

When I was looking for inspiration to start my new series, I realized that I need look no farther than my own geography. I'm a New Yorker, through and through, but the brilliant thing about New York is that being a New Yorker has a diverse set of meanings. I didn't choose 5 books for this series arbitrarily, but rather I wanted to represent the diversity of New York City and its five boroughs: Manhattan, Queens, Brooklyn, the Bronx, and Staten Island, by using each as the setting in a different story. The order isn't significant except that it made sense to start with Manhattan, because it is truly the greatest city in the world. The next book will be set in Queens because that's where I'm from (Fresh Meadows, Flushing, to be exact). But other than that I wanted to tell some stories that all had the backdrop of New York, trying to keep the character and individuality of each borough intact.

Using police as the main characters also made sense, as I've known and grown up around NYPD officers my whole life. Not only is this one of the most famous cities in the world, but it hosts one of the most famous police departments in the world, whose nickname – *New York's Finest* – was the inspiration for the series itself. That said, these are five distinct contemporary romance novels – each with their own characters and their own character – though all the stories are interrelated in some way, which will become clearer the farther down the road you go.

These stories use crimes and settings of the city as a backdrop, not as the focal point of the whole story. These are still romance novels, and the emphasis will be on romance. So forgive me for not going as far down the rabbit hole of true crime that some may crave. I enjoy those stories to, but the crimes and criminality in this series serve as a setting and an inroad to the lives and relationships of the main characters, and nothing else. That said, I hope you enjoy the first of this series, and all the rest to come.

In *Calem*, the first of the New York's Finest series from contemporary romance author Christopher Harlan, a renowned psychologist and an embattled NYPD detective join forces to end the city's reign of terror, finding salvation and love in each other's arms in the process.

Dr. Cordelia Summers is a brilliant psychologist. Well respected among her peers and patients alike, she lives only to help others with their problems. While consulting with her colleague on a case, she realizes that her feelings toward him are more than just friendly.

Enter Detective Calem Walters: brave, intelligent, and a reluctant hero, he's the best the NYPD has to offer. He's worked some of the city's most dangerous cases and his latest may be the worst. His self-sacrificing nature calls him to duty, but he's struggling with the stress of a failed relationship, and the burden of a long chase with one of the worst criminals of his storied career. Can Cordelia help unburden him and help him catch the man who holds the city in his grasp? And does he share her romantic feelings?

A happily ever after contemporary romance series with each book set in a different borough, the New York's Finest series will follow the interconnected lives and loves of five NYPD officers. The events of book 1 take place in Manhattan, with book 2, set for release in the late fall of 2017, to be set in Queens, the author's home borough.

PROLOGUE

The sensation of your fingers on my shoulders is indescribable; a kind of magic that's better felt than explained, but I'll do my best to tell you how you make me feel. A slight pressure—not too much—just enough for you to soften my tense neck, and send shivers through the rest of my body, as though your fingertips were electrified. That tingling works its way down my arms, through my body, and down to my toes, like a river flowing into an ocean.

You know what you do to me, and I can feel the confidence of your touch. I turn around to face you, and we look into each other's eyes the way that we were always meant to: deeply, passionately, and without the boundaries that kept us from this moment before. You don't feel anything but the smoothness of my body, do you? No pain, no tension, no stress at the horrors of this world. No. All you see is me, and all I feel is you.

How did we get here? How did this moment elude us for so long, when it feels so very fated. There I go again, asking questions when I should be enjoying the moment, like you always tell me. You're right. No more asking for answers that don't matter. After all, there's only us.

I reach out to place my hands on your naked chest; the contours of your pecs create a mountain for my fingers to climb, gripping them as though my life depended on it. Below that is your stomach, hard to the touch, but betrayed by the softness of your skin, and the mild film of sweat that's beginning to cover both of us. My fingers explore further, delving downward toward your belt, but you stop me in my tracks. "Not yet," you whisper, your lips only an inch away from my ear, the softness of your breath tickling my skin. I don't ask why; I don't say anything at all, I just follow your lead.

I realize why you stopped me now. You wanted this. Wanted my lips pressed against yours, and nothing else. Your hands go to my face and hold me, while your mouth becomes one with mine, that electricity returning with a vengeance. It feels as though my body is on fire, the aching between my legs growing more intense.

Your name is on the edge of my lips, forced out of my lungs with the rapid breaths of air that I can't help but take. My heart is beating uncontrollably, as the complexity of language vanishes, and I'm left with only a single word to encompass all that my body feels.

Calem.

The only name that there ever was.

Calem Walters.

My hero.

CHAPTER ONE

H e woke up in a cold sweat, but that was nothing new.
It happened at least twice a week, if not more, and despite how horrific it would have looked to someone sharing a bed with him, in reality his screams echoed around an empty apartment. Regrets were a common enough experience, but being kept up at night by a memory that haunted you was another thing entirely. Calem experienced the latter, and it was a pain he suffered in silence, with no one there to comfort him. He had gotten used to functioning with a lack of good sleep; it was an adaptation he had to make in order to keep his job, but that didn't make the nights any easier.

It would be wrong to call them nightmares, because nightmares were occupied with the unreal; full of monsters and demons and things that don't exist in real life. No, what shocked Calem awake to a sweat-soaked mattress wasn't a nightmare, but the most vivid of memories laid bare inside of his unconscious mind. Sleep was supposed to be a respite; an escape from the realities of our lives. But Calem's sleep was a state where his deepest insecurities could perform on a stage each night, and the regrets that he worked so hard to repress were allowed to come out and play before an audience of one.

The dream memory was the same. Always the same.

She was young. Just a girl. Nineteen going on nothing.

She was about to begin that phase of life after high school that adults like to call 'the real world'. And why not move to the city? It was close, more convenient for going to school, and just a few train and bus rides away from home. Manhattan seemed like the most beautiful city in the world, after all; that place where the intersection of all great things existed for anyone to experience. That was what the movies taught her, but the movies always left out the bad parts.

Her name was Amy Jacobs.

She moved to the city with the same dreams and ambitions that all young people had when they came to Manhattan. She wanted to experience the type of life that only the city had to offer: the kinetic energy of human beings everywhere you went; the culture; the food, she wanted it all, and for a few months she had just that. The city was a place of contradictions, though - of dreams fulfilled and dreams deferred simultaneously, and which one you experienced depended largely on the randomness of life, and the subtle choices you didn't realize could be as consequential as they were.

In Amy's case, that choice was getting in the car with him, with the man who would rob her of the rest of her life. He seemed nice enough, but so do most bad men, and when Amy got into his car, never to be seen alive again, she experience the dark side of what a major city could offer. When Calem saw her she wasn't Amy any longer; she was 'the body' - the mutilated and sexually assaulted corpse that had been violated and dumped in an alley like so much trash. That's how Calem met her, and it was her face that woke him in the middle of the night.

She had been his first case as a detective, a rank he'd held for the past decade. What's that they said about first impressions? That they leave an indelible mark on you, no matter what else happens thereafter. Well for Calem, that indelible mark was the look of her body lying in a Manhattan alley; it was the sobs of her family when he had to tell them that their little girl's body had been found; it was the sight of her casket being lowered into the ground.

In his dream she's still alive, and Calem's only a few feet away from the scene where she gets into the car. He tries to stop her, but when he tries to call out, he has no voice. He can see it like he was there, his feet refusing to budge as he tries to run over and rescue her, and his eyes swelled with tears as he watches her fade into the distance, never to be seen again. When his voice finally rings out into the empty city air, she's already gone, and that's when he wakes up, drenched in sweat and screaming her name to his four walls.

That was ten years ago, but Calem never forgot Amy, or the countless others that he was too late to save. He hated being called a hero, no matter how much risk he put himself at, or how many criminals he caught. The way he saw it, heroes save people- they catch the bad guy before they killed the girl. He was just the janitor; the cleanup crew; the intermediary between their crimes and their penalty, passing them off to the machine of the criminal justice system.

Tonight he did what he always did: he wiped the sweat from his brow and face, and took three deep breaths to slow his heart to a normal resting rate. After that a cold drink of water from the fridge, and some more deep breaths. Eventually his body would remember to return to normal, but not before he saw her face once more in his mind's eye. Sometimes before she got into that car she'd turn around and smile at him, as if she were at peace with what was about to happen. Other times she'd curse his name and tell him that it should have been him. But the ones that really haunted him were the times that she said nothing and just stared into his eyes before getting into the madman's car. Those stares reminded him how useless he could be, and that he never wanted to see another face like hers again. He knew that he would, of course, but sometimes to get back to a peaceful night's sleep, it was necessary to fool himself.

It was the Amy Jacobs' of the world that reminded him of his duty; a duty he swore to himself he'd never fail at again.

5

CHAPTER TWO

M anhattan was truly the greatest city on earth.

That was arguable, of course, but what was inarguable was that the *City That Never Sleeps* was everything people thought of it; the place where you could experience just about anything life had to offer, all within a 24 mile distance. Despite its old reputation, New York was a pretty safe place for most people to live and visit. Since 9/11 there hadn't been much in the way of major crimes. That was, until recently. A spate of sexual assaults had gripped the city in a type of terror unknown since the Son of Sam murders in the summer of 1976. And now it was Calem's job to play clean up.

"You look tired," Cordelia told him, seeing the drawn look on his face as they stood at the crime scene together.

"Yeah," he whispered, sounding out of it, "It was a rough night. Didn't get much sleep."

"The dreams?" She asked, leaning in so that no one else in the room would hear her. He looked at her and nodded. It'd been a while since they'd spoken about the Amy dreams, but she knew all about them. As a psychologist, Cordelia knew how critical sleep was to almost every other aspect of life: attention, focus, mood, memory, even immunity. And Calem looked like someone who was on the verge of being sleep deprived.

"Bad?"

"Better," he answered, "but let's focus on this, I'll be fine, stop worrying about me."

This was another victim of a serial crime that Calem and his partner had yet to solve. Whatever her name was, she would forever be the depersonalized "Victim Seven" in all the local newspapers. Strictly speaking, Calem didn't work sex crimes, but this guy - whoever he was- left some of his victims alive and some of his victims like this poor woman in the middle of the crime scene before them. It varied. Cordelia's psychological insight was that the perpetrator was a control freak; he didn't like the ones who fought back, and they usually were the ones who went from sexual assault victims to corpses; always with defensive wounds on their bodies. He liked compliance; he liked the control to do with the women whatever he wanted, and if any of them dared take that experience from him, they usually found themselves the victim of a brutal knife attack. That's how Calem had come to be put on as lead detective along with his partner, Jesse McMann and the unofficial third member of their crime solving trifecta - Dr. Cordelia Summers.

The crime scene reeked. *They always make me want to vomit,* she thought; a terrible combination of death, mildew and other unidentifiable odors that were better left unspoken. Cordelia had worked on a few cases with Calem, but the learning curve in these situations was steep, and she had already gained enough experience to know the awful smell that came with the geography of a crime scene. Gagging uncontrollably seemed a logical option, but she didn't want to project any weakness to the men in the room, so she suppressed the lunch that was creeping its way up toward her throat.

But at the moment the tension in the room was more unsettling to her than the body. She knew all too well that her presence as a woman and a civilian was tolerated at best, and resented at worst. The more time she spent at crime scenes, the more she believed it was the latter. If she hadn't been effective at what she did, she knew the cops would have been openly hostile toward her, but her effectiveness on the other case gave her just enough professional capital with these guys as to have them keep their resentment to themselves.

Dr. Cordelia Summers was a renowned psychologist, a career path that brought her success beyond anything she could have imagined when she was just as a young Ph.D. student living in Manhattan. Officially the NYPD designated her a "consultant" for the department, and unofficially she was Detective Calem Walter's secret weapon. It was Calem who talked his good friend Cordelia into lending her expert opinion and analysis to his hardest cases, and it was for him that she braved the dirty looks and backroom whispers.

Enter Detective Calem Walters.

He was an interesting man by any standards. Intriguing job, good looks, and highly intelligent. He had it all. You couldn't say too many bad things about the guy, but if there was a criticism that held water— one that he had heard from almost every ex-girlfriend—it was that he wasn't the best communicator in the world. He had solved some of the biggest cases of the last five years around the city, but good luck trying to get him to talk about any of it.

At those press conferences with the mayor, he was the guy in the background looking bored; happy to take a backseat to a politician looking to take all of the credit for his case. "Let them have it," he used to tell his partner, "I'm not in this for glory. I know who solved it even if the public doesn't." Calem was weirdly humble for someone so talented, and it made him uncomfortable to be praised in any way for his work. Cordelia made the mistake of telling him once just how important his work was. "I couldn't stop it from happening," he told her. The *it* being whatever horrible crime he was working on. "If I could've, then maybe I'd be worthy of being called important. But I didn't stop it. I'm just good at cleaning up."

That was typical Calem; self-depreciating, curt with his comments, and speaking with a kind of simplistic wisdom that always impressed Cordelia. The one-inch scar on the far side of his face, just adjacent to his right ear, reminded him of his duty to others—a mark that most would shun because of their vanity, but something he wore as a badge of honor. Calem had risen through the ranks of the NYPD relatively fast for someone the age of thirty-seven, mostly due to his ability to close a tough case. Known for his ethics, integrity, and willingness to work however long it took to get the job done, Calem had shot to notoriety for closing a few high-profile cold case murders that other detectives couldn't make headway on.

It was in the capture of a particular bad perp that he earned the battle scar by his ear, and he had nearly lost his life in the process. He was a rescuer by nature, though he detested the word "hero," as most true heroes did. His orientation to police work was on the service aspect of the job: service to the community in general, and to the victims of violent crimes in particular.

It's one of the many things that drew Cordelia to him; that, and his chiseled face and overwhelming stature certainly didn't hurt. The latter two qualities were the gorgeous wrapping on the package, but it was his character that kept Cordelia perpetually interested in him. The origin of their relationship happened like all good things, serendipitously. Their first meeting came at a psychology convention of all places. He was every bit the student of human behavior that she was, though he preferred the grittier side of things to a cushy office. In another life, he might have been a colleague of hers, but as it was, she was the shrink and he the cop. Nonetheless, he considered knowledge of psychology to be one of the most important tools a cop could possess, and he tried to stay current on the state of the field. They hit it off right away, as people sometimes do, and their friendship has blossomed into a professional relationship also.

Cordelia had feelings for Calem ever since their meeting at that conference a few years back, but she couldn't tell if he was interested in her like that, or if he only wanted her for her psychological expertise. Over the past year, they'd become colleagues of a sort; strange bedfellows who had worked together on a few cases with Cordelia in an advisory role. The other cops on the force rejected the idea of working with a psychologist, but Calem had insisted. In some ways he was the archetypal, old school cop: gruff, hardened in his worldview, but he was also open minded and educated, and he wasn't one to give away an advantage that would help him catch a bad guy. And right now, he was dealing with the epitome of a bad guy.

"This is a fucking mess," one of the cops in the room declared. The first case Cordelia consulted on hadn't been this gruesome, so Calem looked over to make sure she was okay, as she peered over at the tortured body. This was something else entirely, and Cordelia knew it. She specialized in the types of disorders guys who did things like this typically had, and her insight might just be the ace Calem would need up his sleeve in order to turn the corner. As she stood in the middle of that disgusting room, something told her it wasn't going to be easy this time around. *What did you get yourself into here?* she thought.

"This is bad news," he said, walking over to Cordelia and placing his hand on her shoulder. "Real bad."

"That's an understatement." The body was tied to a chair, stabbed multiple times, and the ligature marks from strangulation were thick and visible. *Probably a rope*, Cordelia thought. But she wasn't there to do forensics, per se, she was there to notice things that other people might not.

She watched carefully as teams of cops and crime scene investigators scurried around the room like ants, collecting evidence and looking for clues in every possible crevice. She wasn't interested in blood spatter, or an errant fingerprint the killer may have left carelessly. She knew that the cops wouldn't find more than the killer wanted them to discover. He was careful, and that's what she was really there to assess. While the other fifteen people in the room attempted to catch him slipping, Cordelia was there to understand why he had deliberately left the room as he had.

"Any initial thoughts?" Calem asked softly, almost as if the victim was asleep, and he didn't want to disturb her.

"Plenty," she answered. "But I'll keep them to myself for now." She had her own process when it came to things like this, and Calem got that she didn't think like a cop, she thought like a psychologist. He stood right next to her brooding, as he usually did. In a setting that seemed designed for discomfort, Cordelia felt better when he stood near her. It didn't take the smell of the room away, or the horror of the crime, and it only partially muted the voice in her head telling her not to throw up, but it was very real . . . something that he inspired in her.

Calem was a cop, and he mostly thought like one. If you looked up the word *stoic* in the dictionary you'd see his face, but he thrived on personal and professional challenges like he had in front of him now. It was a weird way to think of solving homicides, he knew, but to him the killers were playing a game with the cops; attempting to get away with their crimes; attempting to rob someone of their life and pay no price for it, and it was his sworn challenge to make them pay. He stood staring without speaking for a few more seconds, comforting her with his presence alone, and then the silence ended with the weirdest of questions given the setting they were in.

"Hey, you wanna get dinner after this," he asked her. It was a cartoonish level of disconnect to ask a woman to dinner while standing in a room that would make most normal people violently ill, but Cordelia liked how strange it was, and she found his question a nice break from the craziness and tension in the room.

"Yeah, sure," she said. "I know a place."

They left the crime scene a half hour later, leaving forensics to collect evidence that might help crack the case, and went off to a little Italian place around the corner. "I guess seeing things like that every day desensitizes you a little," she said.

"Trust me," he answered, "I don't see things like that every day. Not even close. But you're not wrong."

"It doesn't bother you?"

"Listen, the day that kind of stuff stops bothering me is the day that I turn in my papers."

"Fair enough. So how would you describe standing an inch away from a murder victim, then asking me to get food after we were done?"

It was a fair question, and as they walked Calem tried to think of how to answer it in a way that would make sense to a civilian. "My sister had a baby a little more than a year ago. She lives in Florida and I was in the middle of a big case when she gave birth, so it took me about three weeks to go and see him. When I got there, she asked me to change one of his dirty diapers and I almost threw up, believe it or not.

It was one of those messy deals where the poop runs up the baby's back and shit—no pun intended. After I asked her how she could go from being knuckle deep in poop and spit up, and then go eat a snack while the kid slept. She told me, 'I'm just used to it.' It's kind of like that, I guess."

"Gotcha. Desensitization, like I said."

"Sorry I don't know the fancy psychological jargon, Doctor." They both smiled, and they got to Pietro's Trattoria a minute later and sat down for a late dinner. "Look, I know that was a lot to take in for someone who doesn't see that sort of thing, so I really appreciate you coming. I hesitated even asking you."

"No worries," she said. "And never hesitate, I'm happy to help. I mean, yes, it was a lot to see that in person, but it's even more motivation for me to help you catch the guy."

"That's an amazing attitude," he said, smiling at her. "You'd be surprised how many cops couldn't even stand seeing what you saw today without losing their lunch."

"Well I'm exceptional," she joked. "But I almost lost my lunch, so don't give me too much credit."

"You sure are," he said.

"What?"

"Exceptional. You are exceptional." *Is he flirting with me?*

"So, what else are you working on besides this?" she asked, changing the topic so it wouldn't be awkward.

"Not a whole lot, but I technically can't share anything with you that you aren't consulting on. Rules and all that."

"Right. Rules. I hate the rules."

"Me too, believe it or not, but they're there for a reason. Oh, by the way, I saw that *TED Talk* you gave on motivation and dreaming on YouTube, that was powerful stuff. I watched it like four times."

"Did you really? That's four more than me."

"You're kidding," he said, genuinely surprised. "How can that be? You know how many hits that thing has? How could you have not watched it?"

"Easy," she said. "I just didn't. It's the easiest thing in the world to just not do something."

"I guess so, but why not? It's still pretty amazing, even if it's weird or embarrassing seeing yourself on that stage in front of all those people."

"It's not even that—although I am more than a little horrified to see what I look like up there."

"You're beautiful," he said out of nowhere, and it was a statement so stark that it almost made Cordelia flinch. You could tell he wasn't used to complementing women, and especially not on their looks. "So I wouldn't worry about how you looked. You looked great." He had never said that to her before, and she felt mildly uncomfortable, if not a little intrigued.

"Thanks. I disagree, but it's a free county." She wasn't being modest, and she certainly wasn't compliment fishing, she just didn't believe that she was as pretty as she had always been told.

"It is," he said back without missing a step. "I'm pretty sure that's what the founding fathers had in mind when they were fighting the British in the Revolutionary War. They were protecting my freedom to think you look beautiful on a *TED Talk* stage." She was intrigued that in the span of a few sentences, Calem had managed to sneak in a few flirtatious comments of his own. She was a student of behavior, after all, and like any good psychologist (or detective), she made it her job to notice things about how people acted. She wondered if he was being strategic in complimenting her, or if he just had feelings for her he was just awkward at expressing. She was exhausted from the day, though, and she didn't really have the mental energy to give those questions any real analysis. But she filed them away in a mental folder titled "For Later."

Cordelia remembered the experience of their first meeting vividly, as though it had happened last night instead of years ago. It was after her own lecture on the nature of personality disorders that Calem first approached her and came up to her and sparked up a conversation. He introduced himself, and told her all about his interest in psychology and how important he thought it was to his own line of work. Oh, really, what do you do, Cordelia asked him. I'm a homicide detective isn't he with the NYPD, he told her, and I use the principals of psychology to help catch the bad guys, but I don't have any formal training like you do. She had been intrigued right away, not only by his interest in her profession, but in him personally. They talked for a few minutes, with him complimenting her insight into the human mind, and afterwards he had asked her to go for a drink.

Who the hell is this guy, she thought at the time, I don't even know him and I'm considering going out for a drink with him? I mean, he's fucking gorgeous, but the whole meeting is a little random and weird. What are the odds a hot, really smart cop who's interested in my field would just approach me and want to go out with me? Those were the thoughts going through her head before, during, and after she said a really quick 'yes' to his offer, and despite the fact that it wasn't really in her nature to do things like that, she wasn't going to say no to someone who made as strong of a first impression as Calem Walters.

The bar had been empty, she remembered. Not completely, but few enough people to make the setting feel intimate. She remembered how dim the lights had been, and how good they made him look. He had these eyes that looked directly inside of her, and she couldn't help but feel uncomfortable at first. She couldn't really tell if those were just his eyes, or if he was looking at her in the way she suspected he was. It was true that they talked shop, with Calem asking follow up questions about all the personality disorders she had lectured on, but he also asked about her; about her education, where she lived. . . Oh, a fellow New Yorker; and about how she had gotten into her line of work. It felt to her like more than just a professional consultation; it felt like a man who was interested in her on a personal level. And who could blame him; Cordelia was no slouch in the looks department - even though she was about the most humble woman ever, she was absolutely beautiful, whether she realized it or not.

They talked for a long time - almost two hours - and she only noticed the time when she went into her bag to grab money for the drinks and saw her phone. Put your money away, he told her, I've got this. She had accepted kindly, of course, and the alcohol had lowered her inhibitions enough where she leaned in and kissed him on the cheek. Thank you for a great evening after a very boring day, she told him. You're welcome, and I'm the one who should be thanking you, he told her. When she asked why, he simply told her, for being amazing. It was then that she first felt something real for him, and even though it would take a long time before he'd admit the same, the feeling was completely mutual.

Their impromptu dinner went on for another thirty minutes before Calem asked for and paid the check. She didn't protest, not that he would have budged even an inch from paying for her dinner. He'd never admit it, but he liked being the hero sometimes, even if those acts of heroism were admittedly as small as giving his friend a nice evening after a shitty day.

They walked outside into the dark Manhattan night when they were finished. Calem had a protective energy about him that always made Cordelia feel like he was escorting her everywhere they went, even when they were just two people walking next to each other. He was a big man, so as he held the door open for her, like a gentlemen, she had to push her way through. In that moment their bodies were pressed against one another, and each of them felt something unexpected. In that nanosecond of time their bodies were locked together as one in the small opening of the doorway, and the pressure of her sliding past him gave him a feeling of excitement that he hadn't anticipated. It was summer, so Cordelia wasn't dressed in heavy coats or sweaters, and as she exited the front doors he could feel the impression of her whole body against his, and in that moment he found himself imagining what she looked like underneath those clothes. He tried to refocus as she finally slid past onto the sidewalk, but he found his mind temporarily incapable of thinking of anything else other than her beautiful body.

Stop staring, he told himself, but there was no helping it. She had a beautiful body, and the more time they spent around one another the more attracted he was becoming to her. It was going to be a busy few days for each of them, but they agreed to meet for lunch the following week to discuss the case some more. He could have just said goodnight and walked away, but he felt an overwhelming need to touch her again, so as he leaned in for a hug he squeezed a little harder than normal, and she did so right back, confused as to what it might mean. They lingered in each other's embrace, hoping that in the dialogue of bodies that was taking place, their bodies would communicate what their mouths seemed incapable of doing.

And then, as quickly as it had begun, their hug ended. *Goodnight Cordy*, he whispered in her ear, followed by a parting of the ways. As he walked from her only one thought kept repeating in his mind again and again. *One day*, he thought, *one day you'll be in my arms longer than that.*

CHAPTER THREE

The Following Week

Cordelia started off her day pretty normally; with a walk to get a strong cup of coffee from her local café. The place a few blocks from where she lived was one of the last independently owned coffee shops around. She hated Starbucks, and Dunkin' Donuts was even worse, so she made the extra trip to get a fresh cup almost every day. She had one of those single-serving machines at her place, but those pods never tasted as good as a fresh brewed cup, and today she was going to need the caffeine. Her professional responsibilities had gotten a little intense as of late. She was swamped with an article that needed editing, patients that needed her all day, and she had to read the online profile that she reluctantly agreed to do for some psychology blogger. Being the modest person she was, Cordelia was less than thrilled to read anything about herself.

She was an introvert by nature, and as humble as a person could be, especially considering how successful she was, by any standards. So the idea of reading a whole article that probably just sung her praises mortified her. The two sides of her personality were the definition of contradiction: *Cordelia* preferred dogs to people on most days, and books to social gatherings on all days, but *Dr. Summers* was a renowned clinical psychologist who had a magical touch when it came to interacting with patients. Even though she could have her awkward moments, she loved people deep down, and her patients most of all.

It was never about prestige or money to her, although her quality as a therapist had led to ample amounts of both. The publications and hefty salary were ancillary, just fringe benefits that came as a byproduct of what she really loved to do, which was to help people with their problems. In the office she valued the interaction, the chance to look across into another person's eyes and truly listen to them. In her opinion the ability to listen was a therapist's greatest tool, and easily the best of her own skills. It was the one aspect of her highly successful career for which she'd accept any praise whatsoever. She was kind of like Calem in that way.

If a colleague tried to compliment her latest publication, she'd call herself a derivative hack; if a student bothered to take time to approach her at the end of a semester to tell her what an impact she had on shaping their career path, she'd thank them awkwardly, then try to escape the situation as fast as she could before turning red in the face. It wasn't that Cordelia was rude, or arrogant, or even disinterested in the other parts of her job that led to such (according to her) cringe-worthy moments, it just wasn't about all that for her.

The coffee place was packed, and as she stood on line she thought about Calem and that hug from their last dinner. They were going to see each other soon and she had him on her mind. She was a visual person by nature, and a lucid dreamer, and as she remembered that unexpected hug on the street, all of the emotions of the moment came flooding back. The feeling of his size as he leaned over to hold her; the fresh smell of his clothes, the slight roughness of his 5 o'clock shadow as his jaw had brushed the side of her face – it was all coming back as though he were there with her now. But it didn't stop there for Cordelia. Where reality had ended, her mind could continue what should have happened.

After he whispered goodnight Cordy, a nickname she absolutely loved and that no one else called her, he moved his mouth down from her ear into her neck. She felt goosebumps on the back of her neck, and that sensation filtered its way down her entire body. With barely parted lips he lightly sucked on a spot that drove her insane with desire. He did this again and again, wrapping his arm around her waist at the same time. She imagined her head leaning back, inviting him to continue, followed by him working his way up her neck until he was kissing her lips. They were so soft in her mind, his pressure gentle yet firm, and she kissed him back until each was so turned on they were about ready to. . .

"Caramel Macchiato!" the barista yelled when her drink was ready. The sound of his voice brought her back from her fantasy outside Pietro's to the very real line she was on at the coffee place. After paying she walked out, calming her breathing down and trying to get back into a mindset to see patients. She pulled out her phone on the walk home to see if the article had posted on the guy's blog. Still nothing.

In a way she felt relieved, even though she knew it was just a matter of minutes or hours before she'd see her face next to a blog post. She had agreed to do the piece when approached by the kid— James—whose Twitter handle was @FreudNeerd27, which made her smile. So, she did what she had to do to stay relevant in her field: she taught undergrad classes, gave lectures (her *TED Talk* on dream interpretation hit four million views on Monday, unbeknownst to Cordelia herself, who barely went online for fun, and never to search for her own content), and published papers in prestigious journals twice a year. But to her all of those things were a means to an end, a necessary set of evils to get real people with real problems to walk through her office doors. That was the job, and that was why she became a therapist.

When clients came to see her, they were immediately taken, as most were, with the architectural majesty of a Manhattan brownstone. She had one of the nicest offices around, which just happened to also be her home. It was an inherited property on the Upper West Side that had belonged to her grandfather, who died when she was sixteen. Much to the chagrin of her sister and brother, both of whom were older than her, the brownstone was left only to Cordelia in their grandfather's will, and she decided to use the space as both a place to live and a place to work.

It made complete sense. Yes, she could have taken her father's advice and sold the property for several million dollars—and there were never any shortages of offers from high-end Manhattan real estate firms to get her to do just that—but the way Cordelia saw it, keeping the property gave her a personal and professional space that was worth so much more than any dollar amount she'd collect in the event of a sale. She regretted that decision from time to time, of course. The idea of becoming an overnight millionaire for no other reason than being born the youngest granddaughter of Peter Summers was a cool idea, but she saw the long game of owning such a valuable piece of Manhattan real estate.

A young Cordelia had moved to Manhattan from her suburban home on Long Island when she was eighteen years old; accepted to Columbia University, among other Ivy League schools that were frothing at the mouth for her attendance. Her parents were against her move to the city at such a young age, but in typical Cordelia fashion she used reasoning and logic to outmaneuver her parent's justified anxiety at sending a teenager to live alone in Manhattan.

From there she excelled, finishing her bachelors, masters, and doctoral work in ten years, which was virtually unheard of. In fact, Cordelia knew a bunch of other psychology doctoral candidates who were in year eight of getting the doctorate alone. At the point at which people could justifiably refer to her as Dr. Summers, Cordelia had shed the baggage of being the child prodigy, and had accepted the more tepid praise of just being a really smart adult, and over the last few years she'd built her private practice into one of the most successful in the city.

A private practice allowed for perks that other jobs just didn't have, the least of which was an irregular schedule that she had the luxury of setting herself. That meant she was free when she wanted to be free. What she did with that freedom varied, but today it was lunch with Calem that awaited her. So, after breaking down barriers with Jessica and seeing two more patients, she was off to Katz's Delicatessen on the Lower East Side.

CHAPTER FOUR

There was nothing quite like a New York deli. Manhattan was *the* place to get certain types of food: bagels, a hot pastrami sandwich, and pizza, though a few people in Chicago tried to argue otherwise. The fact of the matter was that some foods were just better consumed in the city that never sleeps than they were anywhere else in the country. Cordelia embraced all the best foods her home city had to offer, but she appreciated a good deli sandwich like only a true New Yorker can.

She was thrilled when Calem asked to meet her at Katz's, easily the most famous of all deli's in Manhattan, and for good reason. The smell of pastrami—Cordelia's personal favorite—was overwhelming once you walked through the front door, and she was lucky enough to get a seat before the lunch rush began. Calem walked in looking intense as always, and as handsome as ever. It was a strange reaction to continuously have when you saw a person as frequently as she saw him, but she never got used to how attractive a man he was. And that attraction worked on a few different levels. Physically, he was everything she loved: tall, dark, handsome, and in great shape. But past that he was almost the perfect package. He had a great job, was ambitious, scientific in his thinking, and easily the smartest person she knew.

They met regularly over meals to discuss whatever they were working on together, or just to shoot the shit. They rotated places every week, though they each had their staples. It was Calem's turn to choose, and even though he didn't love eating at delis, or anywhere as crowded as Katz's at lunchtime, he knew how in love Cordelia was with their hot pastrami on rye, and her happiness was more important to him than his own comfort level.

"Fucking hell, this place is crowded."

"And it's good to see you too."

"Sorry, I forget my manners when I have to push through twenty people to walk through a door."

"Have I ever told you that you complain a lot for someone as tough as you are?"

"Who told you I was tough?"

"It's obvious. You see some of the worst humanity has to offer on a daily basis, and you still find time to run twenty triathlons, do that *chopsaki* stuff, and be a relatively nice human being."

"Only four," he said, referring to the triathlons, "and that *chopsaki* stuff' you're referring to is called Brazilian jujitsu, and you should come with me for once, I won't bite." Cordelia just nodded like someone listening politely but who has no intention of remembering that name.

"One day, for sure," she said humoring him. "But you've still done nothing to refute how tough I think you are."

"Please don't call me tough. I just do my job."

"We all just do our jobs, Calem. You're too modest; you have to learn to accept a little bit of praise."

"Don't need praise," he scoffed while looking around at the crowd. "I just need to go home at night knowing I tried to make a difference."

Cordelia smiled at the very Calem-esque take on police investigation. "That's a little heavy for lunch, but I know what you mean. I need to have the same feeling."

It wasn't just the case that was weighing on Calem, and Cordelia knew it. It had been six months since *she* left him. The she in question was Tori, the ex-girlfriend, the woman who broke his heart into a million pieces. She had been the girl he thought he was going to marry, the one people speak of when they use expressions like "the one." But like so many other cops, the job had taken most of his time and attention, and even when he was with her his mind was somewhere else besides parties and watching Netflix in bed. He was always at work, whether he was physically there or not, and Tori had reached a point where she couldn't take it anymore. She wasn't a bad person. The few times Cordelia met her she seemed like a very nice woman, but she needed more than Calem could offer, so she left.

Six months sounded like enough time to move on, but Calem felt things hard, even if he didn't show it in obvious ways. He was stoic, but things affected him deeply, and when the woman he loved walked out the door, never to return, it put him in a type of depression he had never felt before. He hid it well to people less observant than Cordelia, but it was her job to notice the symptoms. She had been a one-woman support system as much as possible, but she could tell he was still reeling from the loss of the relationship. "I'm fine," he'd say, on the occasions she asked how he was feeling, half a year after Tori packed her bags and hailed that cab to her new life. "I'm fine." "I'm doing great." "I'm good." All the stock phrases people used when they were the opposite of those things, but they just didn't want to get into it. Every time she asked she hoped he would say something like *I'm fucking terrible, I'm dying inside, and I need help*, but she knew Calem would never be that naked with his emotions, even to her, so she accepted the disingenuous sentiment he offered, even if they both knew it was bullshit.

"Do you ever stop to think we're just fooling ourselves, you and I?"

"How do you mean?" Cordelia asked.

"That maybe we need to tell ourselves that our jobs have some kind of positive impact in the world, or in people's lives, but that really, at the end of the day, it's just a story we tell ourselves?"

"I thought we were getting less heavy with our conversation, not more. That's a large question to unpack over a sandwich and knish."

"I'm sorry," he said. "It's mostly rhetorical. It's just whenever someone tries to tell me how important my job is, I always ask myself what I just asked you. I can't help it. But anyway, what are you getting?"

"If you need to ask that then you don't know me at all."

"Pastrami on rye, of course I know, I was hoping you'd switch it up."

"Why mess with perfection? Answer me that and I'll order something else. Wait, no, I won't actually, forget I said that, but still."

"Why mess with perfection? That's the question?" This time he was smiling, he enjoyed their verbal back and forth as much as she did. "Okay. Thinking something's perfect when it's only good robs you of the willingness to try something else."

Calem was annoying like that. He spoke in short, concentrated bursts of truth that made such total sense that they were near impossible to argue against. But that didn't mean Cordelia wouldn't try. "I disagree."

"That's your argument? You can do better than that."

"Relax, I'm getting there," she joked. "I see your point, but it relies on a particular assumption."

"And what assumption is that?" he asked.

"That there's something better than pastrami on rye. What if everything else on the menu is gross and I tried it all, one meal at a time. Every time I'd have a gross, unappetizing meal I would have missed out on my still-perfect sandwich."

"Okay, now it's my turn to point out the assumptions of your argument."

"And what are those?"

"Well, you're assuming that everything else is gross and a waste of a meal. Odds are at a place this famous and busy there are other things just as good as your pastrami sandwich. But you'll never get to experience any of them if you're chasing perfection."

Cordelia thought about his words, and how sexy she found someone who was her intellectual equal. All of her friends chose guys based on looks alone—which were definitively important—but she had yet to find someone with great physical and intellectual attributes. Calem fit the bill, but he wasn't her boyfriend, something she had to remind herself of at moments like this. "Point taken," she said, conceding his point. "But I'm still getting my imperfect pastrami on rye."

"Fair enough. I'll get the same; it seems like the best thing here."

"You're a dick," she joked.

"So I'm a tough dick, huh? Wait, hold on, that came out all wrong." They both laughed hysterically, so much so that the waitress who came to take their order looked at them like they were crazy, then started smiling herself because hell, what else could you do in that situation? "My apologies, Shannon," said Calem, trying to compose himself and reading the girl's name tag. "We'll have two pastramis on rye, lean please."

"Make that one lean and one regular," Cordelia interjected. After the waitress wrote down their order and walked away a little confused, Cordelia turned to her lunch partner and said, "I like the fat, call me crazy, I'm not the health nut you are."

"Do you realize how many different ways you've categorized me so far? And we haven't even technically started lunch yet!"

"Tough dick, right." She smiled.

"Who's also a health nut," he added. "Apparently, because I don't like to chew on raw animal fat with my lunch. You fascinate me, Cordelia."

"Ditto," she replied. "Now back to the less than fun part of the conversation. Where are things with our guy?"

"You sound like a cop, you know that? Probably from hanging around me for too long. And to answer your question, things have stalled terribly."

"Well you need to include me more. I'm good at what I do, you know."

"Shit, I know that better than anyone, you know it's not about that."

"Then what?" she asked.

"Nothing, really. Maybe just bull-headed stubbornness, but Jesse and I have been toiling hard over everything."

"Is it pride, or are you trying to protect me again? You know I hate when you do that, even though it is sweet, in an old-fashioned kind of way. Is it because it's sex crimes this time?" Calem took a deep breath and looked up from his plate. Sometimes he felt like it was his job to chase monsters; or, really, that all the criminals he dealt with were the same monster: the hydra, and every time he cut one head off another just grew back in its place. He had been the darling of the Manhattan media for catching a serial killer, but almost as quickly as that case had been resolved, a series of rapes began terrorizing the women of the city. He hadn't involved Cordelia as deeply in this case as he had the previous one, and it was for exactly the reason she had just identified.

"Look, I'm sorry, I know that you're more than capable, and that you're the kind of tough that you insist I am. I'll need you soon enough, me and Jesse seem to be stalled." Jesse was his partner of a little over a year; a young kid who was more of a cowboy than Calem was, but a solid cop, and a great balance to Calem's personality.

Their food came quickly, and the two friends and colleagues did what they did best—bounced ideas off of each other over food, enjoying each other's company and working toward a common goal. Cordelia appreciated moments like this, and she was very aware that she had the luxury of enjoyment while her good friend had the weight of the world on his shoulders. When the shop talk slowed down and their food had been devoured to nothing but a slivered pickle and some crumbs on a plate, Cordelia decided to make an offer.

"I know what you're going to say when I say what I'm about to say, but just listen, okay?"

"You don't know what I'm going to say, but go on."

"Except I do."

"I might surprise you, you never know."

"Okay fine," she said, not believing him at all. "You know my door's always open if you want to talk about . . . her." Calem pondered her words for a second. He knew that she expected an outright refusal of her offer, so he waited a few seconds to keep the anticipation of his answer high. It drove Cordelia nuts. "See," she said in a frustrated voice. "I knew you'd say no. I knew it, I'm not even sure why I said anything."

"Because it's in your nature to help people, which I love about you. And I think that's a great idea, how about tomorrow?"

Cordelia was at a loss for words, and stared at him with an open mouth. "Are you okay," he asked "Are you having a stroke? I'm a highly-trained professional, should I get ready to perform CPR?"

"Are you just messing with me, or you'd really come in for counselling."

"I'm not messing with you," he said. "But we'll have to agree to not call it counseling, or therapy, or anything else that sounds too . . . clinical. Let's give it a name, a brand, how about, The Depravity Discussion. It sounds like a podcast or something."

"The Depravity Discussion?"

"People will love it – The Depravity Discussion with your hosts, the renowned analyst, Dr. Cordelia Summers, with special guest Detective Calem Walters. I have this all figured out." He couldn't help but crack a smile as he spoke in his best mock game-show host voice.

"Do you now? Okay, fine. So, our first episode will be tomorrow."

"If that works for you," he said.

"I'll make it work."

"See, we have a natural back and forth style already, our show's gonna be a hit."

"But seriously, are you willing to talk to me. I mean, really talk."

"I have to do something," he answered. "Because my *I can deal by myself* bullshit isn't working for me. I don't feel like I should still be so messed up this far out from a breakup, and to be honest the therapists that the department recommends are shit. So, yeah, pencil me in, Doc."

"You're in. I'm excited."

"I'm glad one of us is. It's easy for you, you get to dispense advice, and I'm the one who has to bare my soul."

"Yeah, it's easy," she said sarcastically. "Like looking at a crime scene and just knowing who did it, then calmly going and arresting the guy. Easy, right?"

"I'm sorry; I didn't mean to belittle your work. I know it isn't really easy. I guess it's just . . . it's really difficult for me to express myself in that way."

"I know," she said. "But you'll be amazed at how it helps. And apology accepted."

"We need to get out of here before I have a full-fledged panic attack from all the people."

"So dramatic, Detective Walters."

"Yeah, yeah, yeah, we can address my dramatics on episode two of our podcast."

"Let's make sure we get good ratings for our pilot episode first before we commit to filming a whole season."

After a few mutual laughs and a hug outside the door, Calem and Cordelia went their separate ways. She was amazed that he had accepted her offer to come in for a session, and it showed her an even deeper layer of his character that she didn't know was there. Things were looking up.

CHAPTER FIVE

The next day saw some of the worst sessions of her career. There was Brandon, the emo teenaged boy whose mom dragged him to therapy after four of his teachers failed him for sleeping in class. There was no getting through to Brandon. Cordelia was good at her job, but therapy had to be voluntary, with both doctor and patient being willing participants. Forcing your sixteen-year-old kid to go to therapy was like forcing a sixteen-year-old to do anything, nearly impossible. Cordelia gave it her best shot, despite Brandon's obvious and maddening resistance to her help. She was forced to end their sessions when Brandon started making up erotic dreams he was having about her.

Then there was Jason, the married father of four who was partner at a corporate law firm in the city, and who could not stop dreaming about killing all of the senior partners at the firm with a steak knife. Cordelia wasn't sure if it was the murderous dreams themselves, or the unmistakable joy Jason seemed to experience when recounting the gruesome and bloody details to her. *Shouldn't you feel bad about wanting to stab a room full of people? Maybe I'm the crazy one.*

After Jason came Sheila, the mother having an affair with her grown son's best friend, who was suffering panic attacks after they had sex. "The panic is a manifestation of your guilt, Sheila. Why don't you call it off with your son's friend and see if the attacks stop?"

"I could," her cougar patient answered. "But the sex is fucking amazing!"

During these sessions it was important for Cordelia to gently remind herself that just because she loved her job, that didn't always make it easy. Thinking every now and again: *It's okay, Cordelia, every job has ups and downs; ebbs and flows; peaks and . . . oh Jesus, enough clichés, every job can suck!* It was true, but that didn't make the countless hours spent with her less desirable patients any more bearable. It wasn't that these patients were bad people, although some were, or that they were a little south of sane, it was that some of them didn't seem like they wanted to put in the work that was required to get better. That was the thing with real therapy, it was work.

Cordelia made it a point to stress this in all of her first sessions with new patients. *Imagine you wanted to completely transform your body*, she'd tell them, *like you needed to lose a hundred pounds, your diet was terrible, and you wanted to get toned; could you imagine doing all that without completely changing your lifestyle, eating, and exercise habits? No? Good, because therapy was the same kind of transformation, only it was a transformation of the mind that needed to happen. But that didn't change the amount of work that was required. So, just like that overweight person sitting down with a personal trainer and dietitian, if you're not willing to put in the work then I'm not the therapist for you.*

She gave that speech within minutes of the first session with a new patient, and how they reacted to her high standards was a critical factor in whether she was willing to see them after that first hour had expired. It was a simple formula that she never wavered in applying to her practice. If a patient understood that getting better was their job, and were willing to put in the time and effort required to achieve that end, then it was, more often than not, the start of a very productive relationship.

It was almost time for Calem's session. She had gotten so caught up in the haze of bad sessions that she had almost forgotten. Sometime in the middle of Sheila the Cougar describing yet another romp in the sack with her twenty-year-old fuck buddy, Cordelia got really excited that it was almost time to see her friend. She half expected him to find a reason to back out, some excuse about working a case and needing to reschedule, but when she got a text two hours before their session saying, "See you soon," she was happily surprised.

He got there a few minutes early, and when Cordelia answered her front door she was shocked by what she saw—Calem in normal clothes! He looked good, too. His muscular build was evident even beneath his detective garb of a dress shirt and tie, but standing there in a nice untucked button down and fitted jeans, the man looked like something Cordelia wanted to jump all over. Calem caught the expression on her face. "What?" he asked.

Shit, my face gave me away—focus. "Nothing," she lied. "I was just happy that you're early."

"Jesus, I hope you're a better therapist than you are a liar."

"I thought I was just your cohost."

"You remembered my branding. Very nice. You're a good listener; this might work out after all."

"Well, it's kind of my job to listen closely and remember what I hear, but I'll take the compliment. Come in." He really did look amazing in regular clothes, not that he didn't look amazing at all other times, but still. There was just something about the fit of his clothes and the way he carried himself that made "attractive" the understatement of the century when describing him.

Cordelia had to make the most extreme mental shift possible as they walked from her front door to her office, which sat adjacent to her living room on the main floor. At the door she had been the drooling wannabe girlfriend, and now she had to quickly transform into Dr. Summers. Going back into the setting of her office helped with that transition, and by the time they sat down to talk she was good and ready.

"I have a question before we begin."

"Oh wow, we're jumping right in, huh?"

"Yes, sir. I start all of my first sessions with the same question."

"Okay."

"Are you willing to put in the work necessary to deal with your issues?"

"Whatever work is required I'll happily do," he said, and she fought the urge to smile. Most of her patients had to think about it for a while before they answered, or they asked "What do you mean work?" But she knew that Calem would get it right away. He was no stranger to hard work. "Did you even have to ask that?"

"Probably not. Habit, I guess. Just making sure you knew what this was going to be like, for real."

"If it's any consolation I've never been to therapy before so I have no expectations, I just know that it's probably a good idea, and I'll follow whatever lead you offer. I trust you."

His words were like a shirt she wanted to have made for all her patients. Listening, hard work, trust; those were the fundamentals of therapy, and she loved that he just got it without having to be preached to. "Perfect. Let's get started."

They spent a few minutes just speaking casually, a technique she employed to help put him at ease in this environment. As the chitchat started to flow over the first five minutes, it struck her how similar their jobs were in a lot of ways. They weren't exactly the same, obviously, but she imagined that Calem did what she was doing when he was interrogating or questioning a suspect. He'd try to make them feel comfortable, using highly trained techniques but making it seem like it was just a casual conversation. Then, when the time felt right, he'd get what he wanted from the person. Cordelia didn't want anything from him like that, and she had no preconceived notions of what he should or shouldn't say, but she was about to step up the discussion to phase two.

"It's that time," she said.

"Shit, it's time already! Damn you give the fastest therapy sessions ever."

"Stop."

"What?"

"You know what. It's time to talk about Tori. Or maybe what I mean is it's time to talk about you."

"Either is fine," he said. "I'm ready."

She had to give him credit, he was thorough. He started at the beginning and told the whole story. He told her how he and Tori met, how much he had loved her, how neglectful he had really been during their relationship, and finally how bad he felt when things came to a rapid end. "And why do you think she left?"

"No mystery there," he said. "I know exactly why she left, she said as much to me. Tori's many things, but shy isn't one of them. If something was bothering her she'd tell me about it right away, and she was never coy about how she felt about the job."

"How was that?"

"She fucking hated it. I mean, she liked the attention I got for my big cases. She liked the notoriety so she could tell her snobby family that, even though I was 'just a cop,' I was a somewhat famous one. But the actual work and what it meant to me, she hated every part of it."

"That's unfortunate," Cordelia said.

"Very. But I'm not here to shit all over her like some bitter ex, even though technically I kind of am. However she felt about the job, the truth of it was that it took almost all of my time and energy, and that wasn't fair to her."

"But she knew you were a cop when you met, correct? That was always the case."

"Yes, we only dated for a little over a year, and she didn't complain about work for a while, until just before the end, actually. And even though it was only a year, I had convinced myself that she'd be my wife one day. Maybe I was just dreaming."

"There's an element of fantasy to all relationships, don't you think?"

"How do you mean?"

"Well," Cordelia began, "what I mean is that there are always things that exist a little more in our own minds than in reality."

"Like what?"

"Like what you just said, for example, but it can be anything.

Qualities that we want the other person to have a little bit more than they actually do; parts of their personality we learn to ignore because we hope the person will change once they're with us. Or, like you said, futures that we imagine even when there's no real evidence that they're ever going to happen."

"Wow," Calem said solemnly.

"What?"

"As self-aware as I like to think I am, it's harsh to hear that Tori and I were never going to have a real future together; that it was all in my mind."

"I didn't actually say either of those things. I'm not telling you that you wasted a year of your life in some delusional relationship with Tori, I'm telling you that we all embellish our relationships with people into versions that we wish they were. You might have married Tori, but it didn't work out. Anything could have happened, it wasn't fated. You could have worked less; she could have accepted that the hours you kept when she started dating you weren't going to change, and she could have adjusted her thinking. Hell, you could have won the lottery, quit your job, and bought an island." Calem shot her a raised eyebrow. "All right that last part was unlikely at best but you know what I mean. No fate but what we make for ourselves."

"Dr. Summers, did you just quote John Connor from *Terminator 2: Judgment Day* in our therapy session?"

"Of course I did, I'll take my good advice from any source it comes from, I'm not a snob."

"Fair enough, and I do get what you're saying, but I'm still messed up about her. I feel like I should be over it by now."

"We never get over it, Calem. What we mean when we say something like 'get over' is that we develop coping strategies to deal with the pain; to live with it; to make it part of our routines until our mind becomes desensitized to it, but it takes a long time to fully go away like you want. A lot of getting over something is actually getting used to it."

Cordelia knew what she was talking about, and not just in the clinical sense. She wasn't a serial dater or career monogamist like a lot of her friends in the city. There had only been one guy worth remembering, and after committing her whole heart to him and agreeing to be his wife, she caught him fucking another woman. That was three years ago now, and as she sat there in her fancy therapist's chair dispensing relationship advice like she was an expert, she wondered if she had any business instructing people how to get over anything. "That makes sense," Calem answered. "But how do I get used to it?"

"By allowing yourself to remember; by feeling the pain you probably do everything you can to ignore, by letting yourself be hurt. Once you do that you can start a process of healing, but I'm guessing if we're still here six months after the breakup, that you haven't allowed yourself any pain."

"I can't," he said calmly, almost as though he were disappointing her.

"What do you mean you can't?" she asked earnestly.

"I mean, if I let myself feel that pain—to be its victim—then people can die."

"Clarify."

"Cordelia, what do you think my job is? The only thing that makes me effective is my mind. I can see things that other people can't; make connections between disparate pieces of evidence; draw conclusions that elude the other cops, that's all that distinguishes me from being average. But if my head gets all fucked up thinking about a girl who left me half a year ago I could mess up or miss something, and that could have dire consequences."

As she sat and listened to Calem pour his heart out while being totally honest, she had two different thoughts. Her first thought was about how stupid Tori was. Not literally, Cordelia didn't even know her enough to make that kind of a conclusion. But there was no other appropriate adjective she could ascribe for giving up a gorgeous, intelligent, and heroic man voluntarily because he worked saving people's lives a little too much for your liking. *Dumb bitch*! Her other thought was about her feelings toward Calem. She felt guilty, as though she were somehow lying to him by sitting there pretending to be only interested in him as a patient, when really, she was happy that Tori wasn't in the picture, because it meant on some level that she had a shot. *Now who's fantasizing?*

"I get those fears, Calem, but I think you're being a little bit evasive."

"How am I being evasive?" he asked. "I'm pouring my guts out to you."

"You are, and I'm really happy that you are, but you need more than just a session of telling your story. I think you're missing something important."

"What's that?"

"You're not okay now. Your mind is messed up as we speak. Even though a psychologist shouldn't say this, if you could ignore your pain and function then I'd tell you to hell with therapy, but the truth is that on some level you agreed to do this because you thought you needed help, which means that you're not functioning at your highest level."

Calem hadn't considered what she was saying, but hearing those very direct words struck a chord in him that made everything seem much clearer. He was being evasive, and he was making excuses that were stopping him from being the best version of himself. That had to end. "You're right," he said. "And you're also fucking brilliant at your job."

Cordelia swore that she was blushing when he said that, but in reality, she just gave a huge smile that gave away her attempts to be totally professional with him. "Oh stop, I have some insight, like you, but I'm far from brilliant."

"You don't have to accept the compliment if you don't want, but it's true."

"I'll accept my so-called brilliance when you start calling yourself a hero."

"So, never then."

"Right, never. But forget the mutual admiration society we're apparently the founding two members of, and let's get back to your issues."

"Issues?" he asked "God, that makes me sound so . . . screwed up. But maybe I am, at least a little bit."

"We all are. I'm not supposed to say that, but it's true. But forget labels, here's what I want you to do. Get a notebook."

"Am I going to school?" he joked.

"Yeah, a really weird, sad, and introspective school with painful homework assignments. "Sounds amazing, where do I sign up?"

"I hate to tell you, but you signed up the second you sat down. To stop you'd have to drop out, and I know you're no quitter. Here's what you're going to do. I want you to write down three things, with a detailed explanation for each thing. Are you ready?" Calem nodded. "First, I want you to write down your most precious memory of you and Tori and why it's your most precious. Second, I want you to write down how you felt when she actually left. And lastly, I want you to write how you think life will be when you finally let her go."

"And when is my assignment due?"

"Well, see, that's the cool part about this school, you get to choose the due date by making your next appointment. But whenever you come back to see me, if you do, I want those three things."

"I'll be back. Of course I will. How about a week."

"Perfect, I'll put it down on my calendar. You can hand the journal in before your session if you like. And of course, we'll talk in between."

"Of course," he said back, standing up and smiling. "I appreciate the hell out of this, Cordelia, I really do." He came over and gave her a huge hug. And huge wasn't an exaggeration; she felt like she disappeared in his embrace. For a second she let herself forget the context of what was happening, and just enjoyed the feeling of warmth and comfort that this hug allowed her. Calem felt it as well. Just like the first time, there was something electric that happened when their bodies came together, no matter what the context. This time the hug was mutual, but Calem held on again. Cordelia noticed a big deep breath. *Is he smelling my hair*, she wondered, and then she did the strangest thing – she closed her eyes. The darkness let her mind wander as it was prone to do; only this time she wasn't without him in a random line getting coffee, she was holding on to him, feeling the rise and fall of his chest as he took her in. *You smell like vanilla*, he thought, *like a warm memory, and I could breathe you in forever*. Then he let go, stealing one last bit of her scent to remember after he left.

"I'll text you later. Get back to work being that hero we both know you are."

"Stop," he joked.

She stood in her doorway, watching Calem Walters walk away from her, feeling somehow emptier for his loss. It was a dramatic thought, of course, they were good friends and she'd probably see him a few times before their next therapy session, but as he walked away she let her mind drift off and only listened to her body, which communicated a single, clear thought that was louder than a shout: *I want that man* was all it said to her.

CHAPTER SIX

Sometimes the comfy bed that awaited her upstairs at the end of a long day was her most prized possession. It was easy to understand why. Beds were comfort, beds were a respite from bullshit and, when it was an especially good day, beds were where the night truly began. It hadn't been a bad day by any means, but Cordelia was tired, and needed to just chill out with a glass of wine and a good TV show. *Can't have just one glass, can I?* An over-poured glass of her favorite pinot noir later, she found herself reclining in bed. It was the one purchase in her whole place that was truly decadent. Even though she had the money to make all of the furniture in her place match the quality of her bed, she just wasn't like that. But her bed was a whole different thing.

She had justified the over-the-top purchase in her mind before she ever even got to the furniture store; a premeditated assault on her credit card that she has never felt bad about. *It's a bed, it's the most important piece of furniture in my home,* she told herself in a rare, unfettered internal rationalization. *If I sleep badly then I won't be good at my job. If I'm not good at my job then my entire patient list might slide down the rabbit hole of mental illness to the point where some may commit suicide, or do God-knows-what . . .* The end result was a bed fit for a literal queen, covered in expensive duvets and bedsheets, which she was currently lying on while attacking her glass of wine.

She couldn't stop thinking of him. Calem. She had him on the brain and he wasn't going anywhere soon. The TV was on, but if someone had asked her what the plot was of that new Netflix showing playing in the background, she couldn't have answered. It was just white noise in the background; something that aided relaxation but whose details could easily be ignored. The wine was starting to kick in, and that lightheaded buzzed feeling that was making her head swim also managed to light her imagination on fire. *No reason to fight it,* she thought. She slid her body under the covers and put the now empty glass of pinot on her nightstand, next to the bottle. Closing her eyes, she let thoughts of him go even deeper, until she was engaged in a full-on fantasy the details of which she would remember long after the TV show ended.

The scene started as a memory from that afternoon. Calem sat on the long patient couch in her office, only this time his shirt was unbuttoned, the sides loosely hanging open, teasing the eventual full reveal of his bulging pecs underneath. His skin glistened; a sexy kind of sheen that emphasized all of the things that Cordelia had already taken note of: the shape of his muscles, the line of his jaw, and all the things that waited to surprise her. He was staring at her in a way that communicated more than his words ever could, which was perfect because Cordelia didn't want his words, she wanted his body. She stepped out from behind her desk, the professional clothes that covered her body that afternoon replaced by only her sexy black lace bra and panties, pulling Calem's attention to all the right places.

She walked over to him, slowly, letting those beautiful eyes of his take in every part of her, his stare making her more wet than she even thought possible. She could feel a throbbing between her legs as she walked toward him; her clit begging to be played with; her pussy soaking wet. It only took a few strides before she was on him. He was still seated on the couch, looking quietly confident, like a male lion waiting for a female to mate with. She stood over him, looking down into those eyes, and from underneath he reached out both arms to pull her down on top of him. She was struck by his strength, somehow overwhelming and gentle at the same time, as he pulled her entire body downward with little effort, and she landed on his lap with her thighs spread over his hips.

She felt his erection pushing into her clit; his eyes never leaving hers. Reaching his hand behind her he placed his fingers around the back of her head and pulled her in for a kiss, their faces slamming into one another passionately, the power of his erect cock pushing against her even harder. She wanted it to do its job, to be released from the prison of his pants, and she reached down to get what was hers as their lips continued to smash together.

With little effort she opened his belt, the clank of his buckle a small victory, and she wasted no time reaching her hand inside the open slit and grabbing on to this throbbing cock. As its girth filed her hand she began to squeeze and stroke him, and he moaned in response to her touch. She kept stroking him, moving her hand rhythmically up and down, still inside his pants, examining his face the entire time to see the growing pleasure in his eyes; eyes that begin to roll back in his head the tighter she gripped. Then, after a minute, he decided that he'd had enough foreplay.

He pulled her hand out of his pants and replaced it with his own, pulling his huge cock out with one hand and reaching between her legs with the other. Moving her underwear aside with his fingers and teasing her clit, she inched forward to put herself on the cock in his hand. He let go of himself and slid inside her wet pussy, and she began to ride, placing both hands on his shoulders and sliding her hips forward and backwards with all the force she could muster. Both of their orgasms growing until . . .

What the hell! Cordelia snapped out of her fantasy to screaming outside her window. She felt disoriented, as if she had been awoken out of a deep sleep, and she was pissed off and turned on simultaneously. She stopped to listen to the ruckus and heard the unmistakable sounds of a couple fighting on the street, followed by her angry neighbor yelling at them to "Shut the fuck up." Ah, New York in summer.

After a minute the couple had moved on but Cordelia hadn't. She was aroused, soaked in sweat, and her heart was racing like she had just crossed the finish line of the New York City Marathon. After taking a few deep breaths she composed herself, still frustrated by her lack of a satisfying ending to her daydream. She was also a little shocked at herself for letting what had been, up to that point, generalized warm and fuzzy feelings toward him to spiral into a full-fledged sexual fantasy. *Well, it looks like I won't just be analyzing Calem's issues, will I?* She thought to herself.

CHAPTER SEVEN

A few days had passed since her fantasy about Calem, the first she'd had like that, and, like all things, she decided to analyze it. She couldn't help being like that; it was a pain in the ass to always overthink everything, but it also made her an insightful and successful psychologist. She didn't want to be harboring some kind of weird, John Hughes like secret adult crush on a good friend, but that seemed to be where she was, mentally. *This is not good,* she thought. I either need to shit or get off the pot, as my dad would say. I need to either say something to him about how I feel, or move on. But now I'm not only his friend, I'm also his therapist. Fuck, how did things get so complicated so fast? I should have referred him to a colleague for his breakup stuff, but now I'm in the middle of it all while harboring some intense feelings for him. I'm a goddam Lifetime movie is what I am.

It was too early to think of the complexities of all that. She still had a life and a job to get to, despite her fantasy from earlier in the week. And besides all that, it was still a semi-normal rest of the week coming up; she had her Intro to Psych and Abnormal Psych morning courses to teach, she had to finish grading some terrible papers, summer classes were the worst, and she of course had to drink plenty of coffee and wine, not necessarily at the same time. And most of all, she was excited that her good friend Haddie, was visiting Manhattan this week.

Cordelia hadn't had a houseguest in forever, but she and Haddie went way back, to their undergraduate days at Columbia, and they had become two ivy-league sisters, each a totally different personality but still the best of friends. While Cordelia went off to her master's and Ph.D. In Psychology, Haddie had always been in love with the arts, and she bounced around from being an independent photographer who worked for different magazines and the *Associated Press*, to being a freelance artist. She was taking a week vacation and wanted to come back home, so Cordelia offered her place instead of an expensive hotel.

Haddie would be there tomorrow, but today still brought with it some things Cordelia had to attend to, the most important of which were her patients. Well, one patient in particular. Johnathan Kenenna was a twenty-five-year-old struggling author who was referred by a colleague. It didn't take more than a few sessions for Cordelia to understand why other therapists had passed this guy around, and, due to her caring nature, she had become lucky therapist number five! That's right, four other therapists in under two years had passed this guy off to someone else, and now the bizarre game of psych patient hot potato had ended with Cordelia holding the bag. She'd been seeing him for a little over a month now, twice a week, which was more than she thought necessary based on his issues, but the guy just loved coming to therapy and insisted that he come more often.

Their early afternoon session started like all of their sessions, with Johnathan complaining about life and generally being unpleasant. The man had a real anger towards the women in his life. He seemed to hate everyone he knew, but the women always came out the real villains in all of this therapy stories. It was 'that bitch' who wouldn't pay him any attention at the bar, or his 'stupid fucking mom' who was always criticizing his life choices, or basically any female that dared not think he was God's gift to the world. Frankly Cordelia was sick of him, and she understood why he had been bounced around to practically every therapist in the city already before ending up on her doorstep. Her sense of pity was already wearing thin, and the more this asshole spoke the less sympathetic she got.

"I'm never going to make it; no one wants to read my stuff. I can't even get an agent to return an email and my family is still pressuring me to get a "real job." This was Johnathan 101: whiny, negative, and unwilling to listen to constructive advice. Cordelia legitimately thought that he just wanted someone to complain to, and that all the non-professionals in his life had surely told him to fuck off by now. He was in every violation of her therapy policies. He didn't want to put in much work, blamed others for what were his obvious personal shortcomings, and, to say it plainly, he was fucking annoying. But emotion had gotten the better of Cordelia's professional judgment—a bad pattern she was starting to notice—and she kept him on as a patient because she harbored some vague belief that she could help him. It wasn't going to be easy.

"Remember what we talked about, Johnathan, you're not just coming here to vent, you're coming here to figure out why all of those things you mentioned are happening, and how you can fix them in order to live a more fulfilled life."

"Why?" he asked aggressively, getting more whiny and worked up like a petulant child who dropped his ice cream on the floor. "I'll tell you why, there's no mystery there, people are idiots."

"People are idiots?" she asked, throwing his words back at him. "Do you think that's a sufficient explanation for everything going wrong in your life, Johnathan?"

"Well, it's the truth, sufficient or not. How am I supposed to help people being morons and not giving my work a fair chance? Am I supposed to build a time machine and get new parents, ones who understand that writing is a real job?" Putting aside the last part which made no sense, Cordelia just listened intently, building a short list of responses in her mind for each dumb point he was trying to make. Johnathan's rants could take a while, so she just let him talk for another minute. "And don't get me started on the women in this city . . ."

"I won't," Cordelia interrupted. "So why don't we try to do something productive now?"

"You don't think this has been productive?"

Cordelia couldn't help but look at him in the same way you might look at a person who squatted down in the middle of a subway car to take a shit. With her eyebrow inadvertently raised and every muscle in her face contorted into the most non-objective *what the fuck are you saying* look, she took a deep breath to keep her response measured. "If by productive you mean a complete bitch-fest, then yes, Johnathan, it's been the most productive session yet."

He returned her look, which was what she hoped would happen. Some patients needed to be coaxed, some needed a gentle approach, and others needed Cordelia to be the detached clinician. Then there was the outlier patient like Johnathan; the asshole who needed a verbal boot to the face to knock him into a rational worldview. "Excuse me, should you be speaking to me like that?" Checkmate.

"No, Johnathan, probably not, but it's nothing to wake up the ethics review board about. On the other side, though, it definitely got your attention, because all you were doing up to that point was not listening to me and ranting about everything and everyone you don't like, and I'm not your friend, Johnathan, I'm your doctor. I'm not here to be a sounding board for your complaints, I'm here to give you techniques that might actually make things better, but if you just come here to rant then you'll need to find another therapist. I know you've been to a few already."

The last part seemed to trigger him into a kind of anger she hadn't seen before. He looked genuinely pissed that he had been told the truth in no uncertain terms. Whereas the other therapists made excuses such as, *Sorry, Johnathan, I just feel like progress has stalled, sometimes therapy works better if you see a different therapist from time to time . . .* Cordelia just told it like it was, unvarnished with any bullshit. Apparently Johnathan liked his bullshit very much. "FUCK YOU BITCH!" Was all he shouted as he jumped up, startling Cordelia as he stormed out of the room, muttering something under his breath. His jolt out of his seat scared her a little, as did his instantaneous rage at being told the truth, and she sat still waiting to hear the slam of the front door. But before that came, one more salutation. "FUCK. YOU. BITCH." Followed by the slam she had been expecting.

What the hell was going on with her life, she wondered. It had been the strangest couple of days in recent memory!

CHAPTER EIGHT

H addie's plane landed at JFK at 10:00 a.m. Cordelia rescheduled all of her patients that day in order to pick her friend up. She hated airports, and for good reason. They were small cities, along with all the congestion, rudeness, and disgusting things that cities brought: large crowds, long lines, rude people, the whole nine yards. At least in the actual city you could get away from people, even if it was in your own home, but at JFK or, God forbid, LaGuardia, you had to do your best impression of a worker ant, huddled with the masses.

When Cordelia saw her friend's head through the crowd she smiled and waved, hoping for some eye contact and recognition. It took a few seconds of frantic waving but Haddie eventually matched Cordelia's gaze and the two friends began to smile and wave like crazy. It had been a while since they'd seen each other in person. Sure, there were texts and Skype, but it wasn't the same as seeing a friend face-to-face.

They were about as different as two women could be, but that sometimes made for the best of friendships. Cordelia was less social, more intellectual, and appreciated the comfort of a good routine. Haddie was the living definition of a free spirit; one of those kids in the ivy leagues that the students in medical, business, or law programs make fun of because they're getting a so-called "useless" degree.

Haddie never much cared what other students at Columbia thought of her, or really what anyone, anywhere thought about her, she just lived her life like the aggressive individualist that she was. If you wanted to go with her on her life's journey, great, but if you didn't, her middle finger was always there, ready to go up and tell you where to stick it.

The two friends pushed through the small crowd of drivers holding signs, family members waiting for their loved ones, and a bunch of other folks until they embraced in the kind of hug that only old friends who haven't seen each other in a while can engage in. Squeezing hard the two women held each other for a good five seconds before letting go and agreeing to get the hell out of that madhouse. Haddie was a light traveler, so they hopped in a cab and headed out to Cordelia's place in the city. "Fuck, this place is nuts, I almost forgot what JFK could be like."

"I wish I could forget," Cordelia joked. "I had to fly out of here for a conference a few times over the last year, it seriously never gets any better."

"And I forgot the never-ending construction that's always going on around airports in New York. I swear to God they've been working on who-knows-what in or around this airport since we were little kids. Nothing looks different to me." The two friends made some small talk on the drive into the city. It wasn't that long of a drive measured in miles, but measured in time it took forever. The end of rush hour congestion, lanes closed for more construction projects, and an accident on the parkway leading to the Midtown Tunnel all made what should have been a short trip into an hour-and-a-half *Lord of the Rings* type journey.

"I think I've aged," Haddie joked when the cab finally arrived in front of Cordelia's brownstone.

"I know, there are reasons you have to be nuts to own a car in the city."

"I also forgot how beautiful your place is. Fuck, I love being home!"

"And I love having you. But I have to admit you'll be the first and only guest at Hotel Summers."

"I'm honored, then. But I'll be expecting fresh towels daily, and mints on my pillow in the morning. Just so you know. I wouldn't want to have to leave a shitty review on Yelp or anything, it might hurt your business and that would be a shame."

"Funny. And did you know I got a bad review on Yelp from a patient the other day."

"People leave Yelp reviews for their therapist? I didn't even know that was a thing."

"People leave Yelp reviews for Taco Bell. Do you remember the world before all this, when we were kids, and if you didn't like something you just kept it to yourself?"

"I sure do, but I try not to. I don't want to sound like grandma just yet, remembering the good ol' days before that pesky Internet came along."

"Shut up!"

"Oh, I wasn't saying you sounded like that. But you did, just in case you wanted to know."

"Thanks," Cordelia joked. "And jokes aside you have to be careful in this world of reviewing and rating everything."

"Can you please stop saying 'this world.' Your old lady impersonation is getting a little too good for comfort. In a minute you're going to tell me about how you used to walk to school in the snow with no shoes, and how kids today don't know how good they have it, with all their mary jane and rock and roll music."

"Can you please go back to California right now."

"Oh you love me, don't hate on me telling you the truth, Grandma."

"If you call me Grandma one more time I'm gonna . . ."

"Wash my mouth out with soap and tell me not to swear."

"All right, I'm done."

"Stop, I'm just kidding," Haddie said, wrapping her arms around Cordelia while they both laughed. "And who would be dumb enough to leave you a bad review, you're probably the best psychologist in the city."

"I don't know about all that," Cordelia said modestly. "But I do know exactly who it was."

"Who?"

"This patient. I hate to say it, but he's a real asshole. The kind of patient I usually avoid."

"So why are you seeing him, then?"

"I felt bad," she answered. "He's been bounced around to four of my colleagues and I felt like someone had to commit to helping him out."

"Yeah," Haddie answered, "and that someone is him. You're good, Cord, but you're not magic, you know that."

What she was saying was true, and Cordelia knew it, but regardless she really hated having negative interactions with patients like she had with Johnathan, even if it wasn't her fault. "You're right, as always."

"Well that goes without saying," Haddie joked. "But, seriously, don't beat yourself up. Of all the people you help on a daily basis you have one crackpot. I'd say that's better than the national ratio of normal people to assholes. You're ahead of the game; don't let it get to you."

"I'll try, I've just never left a session with a guy storming out in a rage screaming 'Fuck you, bitch' at the top of his lungs. Twice, no less."

"He wanted to make sure you heard him. Makes sense." They both laughed again, and Haddie decided it was time to take her friend's mind off the drama of patients. Little did she know she'd direct her into a whole different type of drama. "So, how's the police stuff going? You still playing junior detective to that guy?"

It was moments like they were having for which the expression "from the frying pan into the fire" was made. Haddie could tell from the look on her friend's face that she had somehow touched a nerve, though she had no idea why. "Never mind," she said, seeing the pained look on Cordelia's face.

"No, no, it's fine, I'm sorry. It's just that everything has been a little . . ." She stopped herself to think of just the right word. "Complicated. Let's put it like that."

"Like how?"

"Loaded question."

"Well you know what goes really well with loaded questions, don't you?" Cordelia shook her head. "Drinks. And lots of them."

"Now that's the best thing you've said yet, but we can't go full alchy and start slamming shots before noon. That's a bad look."

"Tonight, then. Take me out to your favorite bar around here and we'll get a little loose." *Getting loose.* That was Haddie's euphemism for complete nuclear annihilation of all the normal rules of social behavior. She may as well have said "let's go fucking crazy," which wasn't really Cordelia's thing. It was moments like that where the differences in their personalities were most clear. But, then again, Cordelia wasn't really feeling like her normal self.

"I'm in," she said to the surprise of Haddie. "But how about we bring some more people."

"Look at you," Haddie joked. "You sound like me, I like it. Who's coming to the party?"

"My friend," she said. "The cop I work with." Haddie smiled ear to ear, realizing the situation almost immediately without any further explanation.

"Your friend, huh?"

"My friend. What?"

"A minute ago you didn't wanna talk about the police work. Now you want to bring your 'friend' to the bar with us."

"So what? And stop saying 'friend' like that."

"Like what?"

"All exaggerated like you're doing. He's just a friend."

"Hey, whatever, it's your business. Who am I to get involved? But I don't want to be a third wheel, so your friend better have a friend."

"He has a partner. Jesse. Great guy."

"Tell me what I want to hear, Cord."

"Yes, he's good looking. Very. And more of your personality type, actually. Kind of the wild young detective."

"Sounds great. Maybe he'll launch an investigation on me after a few drinks."

"You're crazy," Cordelia joked.

"This is true, but that's why you love me. So, set it up for later, but now I'm going to need the Summers concierge service to unpack my stuff."

"You mean those two bags of practically nothing, I think we can manage that. Together, that is."

"Fine. Lead the way."

CHAPTER NINE

"This mothafuckin' piece of shit!" Jesse was angry as all hell. He was still young and relatively new to his position, which meant that he took these cases very personally.

"I agree," Calem said to him. "But calm down; emotion will just cloud your judgment." It was nearly impossible for Jesse to follow his partner's advice; he was a hothead, but that almost made him a good cop. "I hate this fuck as much as you do; this one in particular, but remember how we've cracked all our cases. With objectivity. Don't work yourself up into a lather or we'll miss something."

"Yeah, I know, but it's hard." Jesse had a harsh New York accent and a strong temper to match. He kept it reserved for the bad guys who deserved to be on the receiving end of his wrath, but he was prone to the occasional outburst when a case really got to him. And this one fit the bill. There were levels to criminality; types of crimes that impacted people in different ways, all of which were bad in one way or another, but not all of which resonated emotionally. Thieves were terrible people, violent thieves even more so. Killers were the scum of the Earth. All this was true enough, but there was a special place in hell for sex criminals. Rapists, pedophiles, and all other manner of sexual assault case became a high priority for cops like Calem and Jesse.

Calem hated them as much, or even more so, than his young partner, he was just better at keeping his cool.

The guy they were talking about, the one that was occupying all of their investigative energy was a serial rapist who'd been terrorizing the women of the city for a few months now. So far, the victim count was at four—too high for either Calem or Jesse's liking. Hell, one was too many when it came to crimes like these, but four was a pattern with no end in sight. "He's too comfortable," Calem said as they sat at their desks going over some details. "The fuck is grabbing women in broad daylight, pushing into their homes and raping them."

"Don't forget the torture." That's the part that bothered Jesse the most. The rape was horrific enough on its own; it didn't need anything extra to compound the humiliation and trauma these women would feel for the rest of their lives. But this sick fuck took his time, spent hours in these women's homes coming up with all sorts of depraved ways of making them feel fear. He needed to be put down.

"I don't forget any of it, Jesse, I just handle it differently than you do."

"I guess that's why we're partners," he added. "We balance each other out."

"We do, but we're partners because we're both the best at making monsters like this disappear from society. And that's what we're gonna do. Again."

"Amen, brother."

They sat the majority of the early afternoon looking over details of the case, Jesse getting more worked up with each crime scene photo and victim statement, but trying to keep his emotions to a minimum in front of his seasoned partner. The MO was the same every time: pretending to be someone trustworthy, like a serviceman, a salesman, or some other ruse, this man would get women to open their doors, usually during the day, and push inside their homes. It's most likely he attacked during the day because people felt a false sense of security when it was light out, as if bad things can only happen under the cover of darkness. Once inside he'd secure the door, beat his victim until she couldn't fight back any more, and then take his time in torturing and raping her.

The scary thing was he didn't seem to have a type. His MO was the same every time, but his victim profile was all over the place. His first victim had been a recent college grad with short brown hair on the lower east side; his second an overweight, divorced mother of three; this third a Hispanic grandmother who had just gotten back to her single bedroom apartment from attending Sunday church services; and the latest had been an affluent thirty-seven-year-old doctor. There was no consistency in who was fair game for his attack, so the police couldn't even warn a particular type of woman to alter her appearance, the way women did back when the Son of Sam was stalking Manhattanites. The only ways that women could protect themselves was by being aware of any strange men lurking outside of their homes, and not opening their doors for anyone that they didn't know personally. Other than that, the scary truth of the situation was that almost any woman who lived by herself was at risk.

When the spree started all the usual statistics followed: there were increases in the amount of gun and pepper spray purchases, an increase in home security alarms and security cameras, even an increase in the sale of wigs, with women trying to make themselves look less attractive than they were. But rape had nothing to do with sex, and this guy didn't care what a woman looked like, he'd torture them all the same.

It was exhausting for the two cops to go over all the information; not only because it was upsetting, but also due to the fact that the mayor was facing intense pressure from the public to capture this guy, and political pressure funneled down the chain of command, and results were expected, sooner rather than later. Each new victim would be viewed as a failure, and if there were too many new victims, Calem knew he'd be taken off the case, despite all of the past cases he'd solved. Being a detective in this situation was the epitome of "what have you done for me lately?" and Calem knew that old success would only buy him a little extra time, but it wouldn't protect his job if he couldn't catch the bad guy soon enough.

"We need your psychologist friend, the hot one."

"The hot one?" Calem asked.

"Don't front, Calem, you know she's hot. I've seen the way you look at her sometimes."

"Oh yeah," he said. "And how's that?"

"Like you want to . . ." Calem raised his eyebrow before Jesse finished his sentence, but they both knew what the ending was. "You know."

"Okay, so maybe I'll call my hot friend. You know, for her psychological insight."

"Oh, come on, you know she's a beautiful woman, don't pretend you haven't thought about it."

Calem was torn on that one. It was true, of course he'd thought of it, but that particular *it* was tied up in the complications of his last breakup, his new therapy sessions, and this case, which was most important of all. But Jesse wasn't wrong by any means. Of course he was attracted to Cordelia, and he had thought about her more than once in the way Jesse was describing, but he couldn't act on it, could he? No, she'd never go for it.

Calem heard his phone vibrate on the desk. It was Cordelia. "Speak of the devil. Look who it is, my favorite hot friend texting."

"No shit? That's crazy, I must have some magic powers or something."

"Sure, magic powers. Or she needed to ask me something and it's just a really weird coincidence."

"Nah, I'm going with the magical powers. What does she want?"

"She wants you to mind your business and use your magic to help catch this scum," Calem said sarcastically, looking at his phone. "Huh, it looks like you might be interested in this after all."

"What?"

"Her friend is staying with her for a while, just got in a few hours ago from JFK. They wanna get drinks later at McNulty's."

"No shit? Is she hot?" Jesse asked.

"You mean, does my hot friend have a hot friend of her own, one that's of course interested in you?"

"Yeah, like I said, is she hot? The friend I mean, we already know Cordelia is a smoke-show."

"You think she sent me a picture of her girlfriend? I have no idea. Can you go?"

"I'm there, bro."

Calem texted Cordelia back, and they made plans to meet at McNulty's at 8:00 p.m. for some drinks. *Shit, our next session is tomorrow and I haven't gotten a notebook or done any of my exercises,* he thought to himself. That could wait, and he was pretty sure that Cordelia would understand the importance of this case to him. Or maybe they'd all get so drunk that they'd both mutually decide to reschedule for another time.

"It's going to be an interesting night," he said to his young partner.

"Something tells me you're right."

CHAPTER TEN

The girls got there first, and it was the NYPD detectives who were late, though it was understandable why. They had been burning the midnight oil at work and barely had time to go home and change. Calem thought that he looked like complete shit, and Jesse agreed, but then again Jesse also looked like shit. Regardless, the guys met up at Calem's place and took an Uber to the bar.

McNulty's was exactly what it sounded like—an old-school Irish pub, the kind that were a dying breed in the new Manhattan. So many parts of the city were being gentrified these days. Areas of the city that used to be crime-ridden cesspools were now turning into upper middle class neighborhoods for hipsters. For the past few decades the porn shops, pimps, and low income housing had been slowly replaced with Disney themed stores, tourist restaurants, and high-end shops. Part of that development was replacing the old dive bars of the 1970s and 1980s with expensive spots that catered to a younger crowd. McNulty's was one of the last holdouts from the old New York; a no frills, dressed down hole in the wall that was there for one purpose: to provide a place for you to get fucked up. No fancy drinks, no plasma TVs adorning the wall, and nothing in the way of decorations except some old pictures, a bar, a jukebox, and rows of whatever alcohol you felt like.

"Fuck, is that them?" Haddie asked. Cordelia was sipping her drink, a vodka and cranberry, when the detectives walked in.

"That's them," she said, waving to Calem. "Why, are you disappointed?"

"Disappointed,? Hell no, they're both gorgeous, which one do you want?" Haddie asked.

"You're so aggressive," Cordelia joked. "If you were a few decades older I'd call you a cougar. One day, I'm sure you'll be that mom asking her high school son if his best friend has a girlfriend."

"Um, I'm pretty sure you just called me a future pedophile."

"If the shoe fits." They both started laughing as Calem and Jesse made their way over to the bar. The place was pretty crowded for a weekday night, but then again it wasn't a large place to begin with. The guys pushed their way through the crowd as Jesse yelled, "Definitely hot, holy shit!" He was talking about Haddie of course; his opinion of Cordelia having already been made crystal clear back at the station.

"Hey, sorry we're late," Calem said, leaning in to kiss Cordelia on the cheek.

"No worries. This is my friend Haddie." Calem leaned in and kissed her also.

"Pleasure, Haddie, and this is my friend Jesse."

"He means to say I'm his partner, he's just worried that wording it that way will make us seem like we're married. We're not, I'm straight, I mean, I like girls . . ."

"Good for you Jesse, I like girls too, but only once in a while." Jesse looked genuinely shocked, even though she wasn't exaggerating at all.

Not knowing what to say, Jesse just stuck out his hand and said, "Nice to meet you, Haddie."

"You too, Jess. Can I call you Jess?"

"You can call me anything you want," he answered, trying to fight the smoldering stare that his eyes were trying to give this beautiful girl standing in front of him. There was a booth opening up, so after getting their drinks the four of them sat down in the corner of the place where they could hear each other a little better. They were socializing like normal people from the outside, but internally each was going through something different. Cordelia and Calem were each dealing with their own issues, both personally and professionally. Jesse was trying his best to make small talk and not sound like a total moron in front of Haddie, and our girl from California was the only one just trying to have a good time. It made for an interesting dynamic.

"So, Haddie," Jesse started, "how long are you in town for?" He didn't want to sound too eager, but he wasn't the best conversationalist, and he really didn't know what else to say.

"Right now, for a week, but maybe longer if my girl here doesn't get sick of me." Cordelia looked over at her friend with a surprised expression; this was the first she was hearing of any plans to stay past the week.

"Oh yeah?" she asked her friend.

"Well I wasn't going to say anything until later, but I'm actually thinking of moving back to the city."

"Well, as a representative of the city, we welcome you." Jesse had to throw that in for points, but mostly Haddie smiled out of pity. Jesse had no game for a girl like her, but in a weird way she appreciated his awkwardness.

"I haven't made any firm decision yet, I'm still considering it and I want to see how this week goes. I want to see if Manhattan can still handle me." With her breaking news lingering in the air, Cordelia wasn't sure exactly how she felt. On one hand, it was really none of her business what Haddie did with her life, but on the other hand she knew there was more going on than Haddie was probably saying, and she made a mental note to discuss it with her later on when they were alone. Haddie wasn't the type of girl to just pick up and leave sunny California out of some newfound nostalgia for her home state, so Cordelia wondered what was really going on.

About two hours and a few more drinks later, Jesse had gotten no smoother with his attempts to impress his new friend. Cordelia barely drank at all; Haddie was very close to "getting loose," and Calem was a little north of buzzed. For him being buzzed meant letting his guard down a little, and he leaned into Cordelia across the table and put his face by her ear. "I'm a bad student," he confessed with a semi-drunk smile on his face. "I didn't do my homework."

"Oh no," she joked. "Should I give you detention?" Cordelia was flirting with him. She was a bit of a lightweight when it came to alcohol, so even though she hadn't even finished her second drink she was still feeling it. She was nowhere near Haddie's "loose" phase yet, and she had no intention of getting there. She was definitely feeling looser than her normal self though; the type of loose that let her openly flirt with a guy she was harboring some serious feelings for, but not loose enough to do more than that.

"Detention with you sounds amazing," he flirted back. "Is that my only punishment?" He couldn't believe the shit he was saying.

"That depends on how bad you've been," she said. "I have plenty of punishments I can dispense, trust me." Calem noticeably raised an eyebrow; he had never seen this side of her and he liked it. She wasn't drunk either, so Calem couldn't entirely write it off to the drinks they were having, it was more like they were allowing her to say what she had always wanted to say also. As they flirted they were looking only at each other, like the other two weren't even there with them, and Calem could swear that she wanted him as much as he wanted her.

"Hey, I want one more drink; you wanna come up to the bar with me?" Cordelia nodded and followed him over t0 the crowded bar. The whole place felt alive with energy. It was loud, full of people, and kinetic. Calem had no trouble creating his own spot at the bar, basically forcing his body through the crowd until he had a spot. Cordelia just followed in his trail, and squeezed up against him to not be left out in the crowd.

Between the distance that they were and the difference in their height, Calem caught that whiff of her hair again, and he tried desperately not to make it obvious that he was breathing deeply. He wasn't drunk by any means, but he felt his inhibitions fading from what they were on a normal basis, and he decided to say something.

"You smell amazing," he said to her, once again leaning down so she could hear him in the crowd.

"Thank you." She was blushing, and she knew it. Maybe he'd think it was just her being flush from the alcohol, but there was no covering up that her cheeks were becoming rose colored, and when he complimented her, she looked away and smiled. When the bartender handed them their last drinks, they walked back towards the table where Jesse was doing his best to work his game on Haddie.

They drank and flirted some more almost like they were two couples on separate dates who happened to be sitting together. Whatever Haddie and Jesse were saying to one another, Calem and Cordelia paid no mind. After a while, though, the conversation came to a natural end and it was time to go.

"I'm getting tired," Calem said. "I want to have some energy for tomorrow, if you know what I mean." Cordelia took the hint; she realized that he didn't want to admit he was going to therapy in front of his partner, and most likely not in front of Haddie either, so she just nodded her head in agreement.

"Aww, what's happening tomorrow, the night's still young," Haddie interjected.

"Big case we're working on, have some interviews to go over tomorrow and all that cop stuff. Probably not a good idea to be too hung over." Jesse knew it was a lie; there were no interviews to go over, but he was a good partner and just doubled down on the story.

"Yeah, we need to have our heads on straight if we're gonna catch this guy, so I'm gonna get my boy here home. Sorry to leave you guys high and dry."

"High, yes, but never dry," Haddie interjected, sounding every bit of the drunk she was. "And it's all good; you guys are amazing and need to get your sleep. We understand."

The four of them said their good nights, with each of them in a totally different frame of mind than the other, and about a thousand things left unsaid between them. Cordelia was left wondering what had changed Calem's mood so fast and why Haddie had spent the entire day not mentioning that she might move home. Calem felt bad about his change of mood, and was still surprised by his brief flirtation with his friend, colleague and . . . therapist! Jesus, she was his therapist now, wasn't she?

Outside Calem and Jesse stood, waiting to hail a cab and feeling a little shaky after having just stood up after a few too many. "What was that all about?" Jesse asked.

"Not now, man," Calem said, not wanting to discuss anything.

"All right, whenever you're ready."

"Yeah, anytime but now. Right now, I just wanna go home and sleep it off."

"That sounds like a great idea. Haddie's cool, man. I didn't know what to say to her to save my life, but I really liked her."

"Yeah," Calem agreed, lost in his own thoughts of Cordelia. "She seemed really cool, you should ask her out sometime."

"Maybe I will. But I want to give it some time. I don't think I made the best first impression, but she was nice about it."

"Impressions are funny things, man. Sometimes the idea you have of a person is all wrong. You think a person is one thing to you, but they turn out to be something else entirely. You just never know."

Jesse didn't know what the hell his partner was talking about, and it sounded just like the incoherent ramblings of a drunk guy, so he just nodded his head and waited quietly for the cab. It was a weird night.

CHAPTER ELEVEN

C alem woke up with a splitting headache.

He probably should have expected to be hung over. Three drinks might have barely constituted a warm up for your average college kid, but for someone who lived as cleanly as Calem did, it was a shock to his system. He hadn't had a real hangover in years, and as he opened his groggy eyes to look around a room he barely recognized, the throbbing sensation in both temples pounded in perfect rhythm like a metronome. *Fuck, I need Tylenol, or Advil, or a fuckin' bullet to the head to put me out of my misery.* "Happy morning, partner," Jesse said, which sounded to Calem like someone yelling into a megaphone pointed directly at his ear.

"Jesus, man, you don't have to yell."

"I'm not," he said. "Shit, man, how much did you have last night? You look half dead."

"Too much," he said, gripping his temples. "At least for me." Calem wouldn't have classified himself as a health nut like some others had called him, but he was definitely health conscious. He trained in martial arts his entire life, ran marathons and triathlons, and generally felt happier when his body was optimized for performance. That meant taking only healthy things into his body, and he was pretty rigid about it. He wasn't one of those judgmental health snobs who told other people what they were eating was crap, but for his own diet he liked to keep it strict.

He ate only organic produce. He hunted elk twice a year so he could have his own meat supply without hormones or whatever else they gave to those poor animals at slaughterhouses; he ate fermented foods like kimchi and sauerkraut, and generally avoided processed foods. That also included not drinking much, and never doing drugs, so a night of some light drinking felt like a full-out frat party kegger to him. He was paying for it now. "I need something for my head."

"You need more than that, we have to train."

"Oh fuck," Calem said. "I totally forgot."

Wednesdays were packed for him. He had his therapy session with Cordelia at noon, and work after that, but the morning was for training. "Forgot?" Jesse asked. "Well, I guess that makes sense considering how messed up you are, but we're going, my friend. You dragged me to this Jiu-Jitsu stuff, so there's no way I'm going alone now. So, here." He handed Calem a bottle of water and two Tylenol. "Take these, we have an hour, so you should start to feel better by then. Drink some water. Actually, drink lots of water."

It was good advice, and even though Jesse was hurting a little bit himself, his body was much more accustomed to being filled up with alcohol and then functioning the next day. Training was going to be hard, Calem thought. It's hard on a normal day, but it was going to be torture today. And then therapy, that's going to be hard also and then there's the case afterwards. *Fuck this day, it's only 8:00 a.m. and I'm already done.*

An hour later they arrived at a Rodrigo Silvia's Brazilian jujitsu, bags in hand and headaches in temple. BJJ was a grappling art, like wrestling or judo, only it was focused on self-defense and submitting to a larger and stronger opponent through leverage and joint manipulation. Calem was a four-stripe brown belt—the last step before black, which was a rare accomplishment. He had been training for the better part of eight years, and in the state he was in the idea of rolling around with two-hundred-pound monsters was daunting, but he knew it had to be done. He had dragged Jesse there when they became partners. Calem believed that it was a cop's duty to know how to handle himself and subdue a perp when necessary, and it was a sunk in rear naked choke—a basic BJJ move—that had allowed him to catch many bad guys who were trying to hurt him.

In the changing room Calem was still feeling the effects of last night. Five hundred milligrams of Acetaminophen and a sixteen-ounce bottle of mineral water wasn't exactly a medically sound solution for the toxicity his body was still experiencing. He knew that nothing but some time and more hydration would make him feel normal again. "Next time we get invited to something like that, it's a beer or water for me, don't ever let me drink that much again."

"For the toughest guy I know, you're pretty weak when it comes to stuff like that," Jesse answered.

"I'm not tough."

"Okay. And I don't like attention or pretty women."

That one made Calem crack a smile. "And anyhow, it's not about being tough. I don't know what that means, it's just about persevering, and doing what's important even when you don't feel like it, no matter what."

"I hate to tell you, partner, but that's being tough. Tough is just easier to say then 'you're the most persevering man I know who always does what's important even when you don't feel like it.' That doesn't really roll off the tongue. 'Tough' is just easier. Now, come on and get changed."

While they put on their Gi's and belts Jesse remembered that little exchange between Calem and Cordelia the night before, and figured he'd bring it up. "So, what was that shit you said about having a big day, today? Were you just trying to get us out of there, because I was turning a corner with Haddie."

"Oh yeah, and what corner would that be? 'Cause I didn't see anything but her drinking and you saying awkward shit. If that's the corner you mean, then yeah, you were turning it all right."

"Don't change the subject; I'm talking about you and Cordelia. What was that about needing to get going because we had a big day with our case? Interviews or something? As far as I knew it was just a normal day." Calem didn't know how to handle this one, and quite frankly he had forgotten that he said that in front of everyone last night. All he remembered was a little flirtation, thinking of his ex, and wanting to get the hell out of there.

"Look," Calem began, "I didn't want to make a big thing out of this, and I sure as shit didn't want to announce it in front of everyone last night, but I've been seeing Cordelia."

"Woah, woah, woah, you're dating her now? Why the hell didn't you tell me?"

"No, not 'seeing' like dating, 'seeing' professionally. She's my therapist."

"Therapist? Why do you need a therapist? Everything all right?"

"Not really, man," Calem admitted. "The truth is I've been off my game since Tori hit the road, and between that and a bunch of stressful cases in a row I don't feel like myself on most days, I fake my way through a lot of it."

"Fuck, man, I had no idea. Why didn't you tell me?"

"Maybe I am too tough for my own good like everyone says, I don't know." They both smiled, and there was a lot of truth to that statement. Calem was hard-nosed, and his default mode when it came to anything difficult or challenging was to bite down on his mouthpiece and move forward, never stopping until he got the job done. That's what collegiate wrestling had taught him, and that's how his brain was wired. But mental health issues weren't something you could gut out, and the depression he was feeling couldn't be worked through like everything else in his life could.

"You could have told me, you know, you don't have to be embarrassed or anything. It's the people who don't get help for themselves that I'd judge, not the ones who do."

"Thanks, man, I appreciate it. This case has my brain all twisted."

"Me too. And you know why."

"Yeah," Calem said. "I know why. But we don't have to get into that right now."

"No. Right now we need to go tap some bitches and sweat that hangover out on the mats."

"Please don't say 'tap some bitches' in front of anyone but me. Especially since you're the lowest ranked belt here right now, so in all likelihood you'll be said bitch. Get your fingers ready."

"Just for that I'm not going easy on you."

"Jesse, my friend, I may still be half drunk, but I'll still take your arm home with me."

"Let's do it."

CHAPTER TWELVE

Training was harder than anticipated, and Calem made a promise to himself to never be in a position where he'd be vulnerable on the mat like that again. *Shit, Jesse almost caught me in a submission, which would be embarrassing, but I got out and reversed it quickly enough.* Despite that little near disaster, Calem felt unburdened by telling his partner that he was seeing a psychologist. After all, there was no stigma to that sort of thing like there used to be. He wasn't Tony Soprano; he didn't live in a world where expressing negative feeling and seeking help would be perceived as some sort of weakness, and he really didn't know why he hesitated to tell his partner. It was true some cops were old school and didn't believe that you need to talk about your problems to a professional, but he didn't give a shit what those people thought. And now it was out in the open, and even though his body and his head hurt something awful, he was on his way to Cordelia's with his pride intact.

After making a quick stop at his place for a shower after training, he decided to walk to Cordelia's, he had some thinking to do. His brain was his best asset, but most of his thinking revolved around problem-solving and analysis of crimes; he wasn't the most introspective of people when it came to his personal life, and he was hoping Cordelia would help him with that. In fact, he knew that she would. The problem was that part of the personal issues he needed to work through seemed to involve her. Jesse was right; Cordelia Summers was one of the most beautiful women Calem had ever seen. She was brunette, skinny, and had a type of intelligence that was rare. If he was being honest with himself, he was very attracted to her.

The problem with that attraction was twofold: first, he was still hung up on his ex, Tori, which was partially why he was going to therapy to begin with. Secondly, because of that therapy and the work they collaborated on for the NYPD, he and Cordelia were locked in this weird, semi-professional relationship that complicated him just asking her out. He wasn't shy when it came to women, and if things were different, and she was just some woman he met at a bar, the whole situation would be much simpler. Then there was a third problem; he really couldn't tell if she was interested. They'd known each other for a while, and spent countless hours in each other's company, both personally and professionally, but nothing had ever happened. Maybe that was a sign. Or maybe she was waiting for him to make the first move. *Jesus, why were things never easy when it came to women!*

When he made it to her place he saw that Cordelia was waiting for him on the steps that led up to her front door. Well, not exactly waiting for him, but just waiting outside. The city could be a giant sauna in the summertime, but today there was almost no humidity, and there was a nice breeze flowing through the streets. It was sunny, but not the type that made you want to run inside and sit in front of the A/C, and it was early enough in the day that the mosquitoes hadn't invaded the area like a marauding army.

Cordelia had her headphones on and she was using a meditation app that Haddie had recommended. So far it wasn't working worth a damn. "It's strange to see you with headphones on, you know that?"

"And why is that?"

"I don't know, it makes you look . . . I mean, you look good, it's just out of character."

"Out of character?"

"Would you please stop repeating my every word like some shrink in a movie."

"Shrink?"

"All right, I've had enough." She cracked a smile to let him know she was only joking, and took her headphones off.

"There, am I back in character now?"

"Much better."

"Good. And I'm not listening to music, by the way, I'm doing some meditation thing I downloaded this morning. Trying to declutter my stress, or however Haddie put it. Something about being mindful, I don't know."

"And how's that going?"

"Terribly, but I didn't expect one fifteen-minute app session to fix my problems. I'll give it another shot later on, just figured it's better to be out here on such a beautiful day. I think the weather's helping my mood more than the app guy speaking softly in my ear."

"I understand that, I walked from the station for that reason. We don't get too many days like this."

"That's ten city blocks, how are you not sweating?"

"I left my sweat in bed from all the drinking, and the last bit of it on the mat with Jesse this morning. My body's conserving everything else to help this headache go away."

"Your knowledge of human physiology is amazing. I'm surprised med school didn't call you over the police academy."

"Well that's a crazy story," he joked. "When I got the acceptance letter from Harvard medical school I just ripped that shit up. They took too long to respond, so fuck them. Their loss was the NYPD's gain. Better to chase maniacs and criminals around the city."

They both laughed their sarcasm off and headed inside for what both of them knew would be a much more serious conversation. Calem was ready for it, though; he knew that nothing could feel worse mentally than he was already feeling physically. He took his seat on the fancy patient couch and they began. "So, look, I have to apologize about last night, and about not doing the journal assignment, I have no excuses except being swamped at work."

"It's not a big deal; we can discuss some of it today, or whatever you want to talk about, but what about last night? Did something happen?" Cordelia was being uncharacteristically coy, she was buzzed last night, for sure, but she hadn't been anything near drunk, and she remembered the night perfectly. She knew what Calem was referring to, but she wanted him to say it first.

"It was nothing much, but I felt like we were . . ." He stopped himself. He honestly thought he'd be coming here to discuss his ex and whatever else was bothering him, and right away he was about to say something about their flirting last night, but he stopped himself. "I feel like my mood changed all of a sudden, right at the end before we left, and I didn't' know if it came across weird or not. I didn't mean to cut the night short, I just had a lot on my mind."

"Nothing to apologize for. I was getting tired and Haddie was getting too loose. I should thank you, actually, because if you hadn't cut things off I would have had to hold her hair back all night. Plus, I would have had to listen to more of Jesse's horrible pickup lines."

"They're terrible, right?"

"We were laughing about it the whole way home. Is he always like that with women?"

"No," Calem answered. "Actually, I've seen him be much smoother than that, and he's had girlfriends on and off since we've been partners. Nothing serious, but I've never seen him talk to anyone like that. Must be an effect Haddie has on guys."

"She's got a lot of effects on guys, but that's a conversation for another day. We're here to talk about you. How have you been feeling over the last week or so?"

"Honestly, kind of the same as I was feeling before. Not that I expected some miracle cure from a short conversation, but not a whole lot has changed."

"Don't expect it to right away, and I'm not mad about the journal thing, but it's a technique I use all the time with patients because it actually does help if you stick to it, but that's on you."

"I know, you're right. I'll do it this week, for sure. Since I still need to work on that, can we talk about something else?"

"As long as you're not avoiding dealing with feelings about Tori, then absolutely. Let's make a deal, by next week's session you'll come back with that journal filled out. If you don't have time to get a notebook then do it on your phone, or on paper at home, whatever, but get it done."

"I will," he agreed.

"What did you want to talk about?"

"The case we've been working on. The rapist."

"Yeah, I'm sorry I haven't been as much help as I could have been, I've been swamped also."

"No, it's fine, it's not your job, and I appreciate your insight when you can give it. That's not what I wanted to talk about."

"Then what?"

Calem hesitated for a second before answering because he wanted to word how he was feeling just right. He wasn't used to being vulnerable on a regular basis. "The case is breaking me, Cordelia. I stay up thinking about it . . . Obsessing about it, really, and this guy is attacking women so frequently I feel like I'm already responsible for all of his future victims if I don't catch him soon. And on top of my own guilt, my boss is coming down on me hard to get results, and it's all getting to me."

"I understand all of that, it makes perfect sense," Cordelia said in a soft voice. "That kind of internal and external pressure would get to almost anyone, not just you. But you have to stop thinking that you're responsible for anything. You aren't. Your job is to stop men like him, whoever he is, but you're not responsible for his actions, only he is. You can't save the world, Calem, you can only do damage control."

Calem had never heard it said exactly like that before, and something about the way she articulated her points made it very clear to him. "I know you're right intellectually, but I still feel a weird responsibility," he continued. "Because if not me, then who?"

"I hate to tell you this, but everything you do is finite. Our jobs, our ability to help, even our lives. Everything only lasts for a set time period, whatever that may be. There were thefts and rapes and murders in the city long before you joined the force, and I hate to tell you, but all those things will still happen after you retire, no matter how long you work or how many guys you take off the street."

"I know you're right in what you're saying, but if I thought about my job the way you're describing it I would feel like nothing I'm doing actually matters. It's too detached for me."

"Don't misunderstand me; everything you do matters, Calem. The city is better for you being on the force then if you were a librarian or something, but that doesn't make you Superman. Every person who won't be killed, or robbed, or extorted because of a bad guy you put away, that makes you a hero, whether you call yourself that or not. But that doesn't mean you have the right to beat yourself up and put unreasonable expectations on yourself, and it sure as hell doesn't mean that you should take on personal responsibility for any criminal's actions. That's why you're feeling excessive stress. You're beating yourself up."

Hearing her words was difficult, but somehow comforting. On some level, he didn't want to accept what she was saying, but he also knew that it was the truth, and that it was only his ego blocking him from accepting everything she said. She was right, it's not his fault that some guy is assaulting women, and the scary truth is that even if he was caught tomorrow he'd be replaced with another sex offender the next day. But even if he accepted that his job was a game of bad guy whack-a-mole, he still needed to play that game with all of his energy and effort. "Maybe I should download that app you were using," he joked.

"You should, Haddie swears by it, but she probably uses it much more than I have so far. Give it a shot. But do you understand where I'm coming from?"

"Yeah," Calem agreed. "I do get it, and I appreciate what you're saying, I just have to work on not beating myself up, basically."

"Exactly. Work your hardest, but allow yourself some room to breathe."

"Speaking of room to breathe." He ignored it when it rang earlier because he didn't want to be rude, but when his cell dinged for a second time he knew he had to attend to it. He only used that cell for work, and only a select few even had the number. Apologizing to Cordelia, he pulled the phone out of his pocket and unlocked the screen. The dark look that overcame his face shocked Cordelia.

"What is it?" she asked.

"Tell me again how I'm not responsible for the world's criminals."

"You're not, but why, what happened?"

"Another girl was attacked late last night, and now I have to go."

The New York News

Another Manhattan woman became the victim of the serial rapist the police have yet to apprehend. The woman, whose name is being kept confidential out of respect for her privacy, is currently being treated at New York Presbyterian for her wounds, and is in critical condition.

Like the other women, last night's Jane Doe was the victim of a push-in by a man purporting to be a police officer. According to eye witnesses who saw their verbal interaction before he entered the home, the perpetrator was dressed in "convincing" NYPD blues.

The man is known to break into his victim's homes, typically women who live alone, in broad daylight, using the ruse of being a serviceman of some sort. He then tortures and rapes his victims before leaving them for dead. So far no eye witnesses or victims have been able to describe the man's face with any consistency, and it's believed he might use some technique to mask his true facial features, but this is only speculation at this point.

More details will be released as they become available.

CHAPTER THIRTEEN

C ordelia didn't realize just how bad it was going to be when she saw Calem again, but she knew that it was unusual for him to have asked her to *squeeze him in* the day after their last session. He had stormed out in a hurry after getting a notification that another woman had been attacked by the Manhattan rapist, and she hadn't spoken to him since, until his frantic call the following day. "Tomorrow, after work, just come by," she replied.

That day she taught a class in the morning, did a short phone interview for an online psychology magazine, and was currently having lunch with Haddie. She hated framing it like this, but it'd been a whirlwind of a week since Haddie landed. None of it had to do directly with her, of course, but her arrival had been a little bit of a benchmark to some craziness taking place in everyone's life. But today her presence offered some respite from the crazy. Haddie wanted to get out, as usual, and Cordelia needed a nice meal with a friend before dealing with what was surely going to be a stressed out Calem. They went to a little outdoor place they used to eat at when they were still students at Columbia.

"Tell him to meditate," Haddie said when she heard about the whole Calem thing.

"I did, and I shouldn't have even told you that, it's a complete violation of doctor-patient confidentiality. I could lose my license."

"Yeah, if I reported you, which I'm not doing. We're just two friends talking, so let the guilt go."

"Which one of us is the therapist, again?"

"Well, you're the trained one; I'm the girl who's just prone to giving solid advice and making people feel better. Not really the same level, but I have my moments here and there. I'm starving by the way."

"Me, too, let's order."

The two friends enjoyed a meal relatively free of any drama talk; no ex boyfriends, no work stress, and past that first few exchanges, no Calem stuff either. But there was still one thing Cordelia wanted to bring up, but she waited until they were almost ready for the check. "So, that thing about moving back home? What's the deal with that? How come you didn't mention it to me before?" Haddie looked up from her plate of pasta and smiled as though she'd been waiting for the question for a couple of days.

"I really thought you were going to ask me yesterday."

"Forgot. I've been busy, as usual."

"I forgive you. And, yeah, California wasn't working out, to be honest. My photography business was running dry, the guys there sucked, and I just felt like there was nothing there for me anymore. All my old friends and family are somewhere in the five boroughs, so I was thinking of making New York my home again. Or at least giving it a try."

"I think that's great," Cordelia said, genuinely happy for her friend. Haddie smiled in an almost surprised way.

"Oh, wow, thanks," she said. "I thought you were going to tell me I was making a mistake."

"I'm not your mom, Haddie, and even your mom isn't judgmental like that if I remember her correctly. If this is a mistake then you'll find out for yourself, but I think it's brave to up and leave the place you've lived for years and start over. You know I'll help you with anything you need to make that process easier."

"Well, now that you mention it . . ."

"There it is," Cordelia joked. "I knew you'd have this all set up and planned out in your head."

"Hey, I know you have me pegged as the hippie, free spirit chick, which I totally am, but I'm a modern-day hippie. I'm savvy and I'm a big believer in showers and shaving, I just don't like being tied down. And all I need is to be able to stay with you until I find a place, but not in an open-ended way, I've been looking since before I even got here, but places are just really expensive."

"Yeah, tell me about it. Why don't you try Queens? It's still close to the city and parts of it are much less expensive than where I am, you could get the best of both worlds if you look carefully. I can help you with that; I have a few friends who are in real estate in this area."

"That would be amazing, thank you. And I can be a Queens girl."

"I can see you in Queens, for sure."

They ate for a few minutes before Haddie brought up the elephant in the room. "So. . .you and Calem, huh?"

"Wait, what?" Cordelia asked, more shocked that Haddie's question came out of nowhere than at the topic she brought up.

"You heard me. If you think I didn't see how you two were with each other at the bar you're crazy."

"You noticed that?"

"Cord, I love you, but a subtle flirter you're not. But it wasn't just you basically offering to whip him that I noticed."

"What was it then, I'm curious."

"Ah-ha, see, I was right!" Cordelia had to nod, she couldn't deny it any longer, plus it felt good to be able to talk about the whole Calem thing with a friend. "It wasn't any words, exactly; it was actually how he looked at you."

"And how was that?"

"Like he was a man starving in the desert and you were food," she joked. "He looked at you like he wanted you more than anything else in the world. It's hard to explain – it's the intensity in his eyes; the way he found ways to reach over and touch you as we talked, or how he was undressing you with his eyes. It was everything"

"Huh." Cordelia was buzzed, but she'd noticed most of what

Haddie was describing. She was always doubting Calem's gestures towards her because everything up to the other night had been little, subtle things: a brush of bodies, a little comment about how beautiful she was, or how good she smelled; an embrace that lasted a little longer than it needed to on both sides. In each case Cordelia had noticed all these things, but she second guessed what they meant based on her own feelings. *You're reading into everything because you're into him,* she'd think, *that was just a hug, or a friendly compliment, nothing more.* But now that Haddie was corroborating all of it, she started to believe that her intuitions had been right all along.

"I'm so glad we're talking," she told her good friend. "I thought I was just being a stalker in my head."

"If anything, he's stalking you, Cordelia. Trust your intuition, it isn't wrong. If you feel a guy's into you, he probably is. It's the guys who usually mistake friendliness for attraction, not the other way around. Women know the difference, and trust me, he wants you bad. The only question is what you're going to do about it."

Do about it. That expression intimidated Cordelia more than she let on. That was the missing piece of the puzzle. Feelings were one thing; flirtations were another, but acting any further than that was a whole different ballgame. "That's easy, I'm not."

"Oh, come on, are you kidding me? You have a hot guy who is obviously into you, and you're going to pretend like you're just colleagues? How can you do that?"

"Listen, I know you're the girl who will just bite the bullet and ask a guy out, or make the first move of any kind, but that's 100% not me – it's not most women."

"I'm special, I know," she joked. They both smiled. "But seriously, I'm not saying take off your clothes and jump on the guy, though that's not a bad idea altogether."

"Yeah, not happening, next suggestion."

"What I really meant was maybe you could let him know that you're receiving his messages; encourage him a little bit, you know? Nothing crazy. Let him be the man and make a move if he wants to, but find ways to let him know you're into him also. That's all."

"I'll work on that," she said. "In the meantime let's pay this check and get out of here. I appreciate your advice, Haddie, I really do, even if it's hard for me to actually put into practice."

"That's what I'm here for."

Cordelia picked up the check without thought; she knew Haddie was hurting for cash, especially after everything she just said about her business falling apart, so paying for lunch was something she was more than happy to do. What she was less happy to do was see Calem, who she knew would be a mess, plus she had patients before him. So, after paying the check, the two friends hit a few stores in the area before heading back home.

Haddie was going out that night. She was that girl who could just go out by herself, meet a bunch of people who would become good friends, and have a night that would go down in history. And as much as Cordelia loved her old friend, she was happy at the idea of just having some introvert time to sit and read, or do whatever without having to entertain a houseguest.

In a nice change of pace, the patients Cordelia saw before Calem were two of her favorites. There was Beth, the divorced mother of two who wanted to get out and date but suffered from intense anxiety, and then there was Michael, the college kid whose depression was stopping him from getting the grades he wanted. Both of them were great people who were some of the most coachable individuals Cordelia had ever counseled. They were open, they listened to advice, and they didn't shy away from hard work, so the two hours before Calem got to her were pleasant. She hadn't heard back from Johnathan Kenenna since he stormed out cursing her name. He was supposed to come in today but missed his timeslot. The way she figured it, he had unofficially left her to find therapist number . . . who even knew anymore? *Good riddance,* she thought. *Go be a pain in the ass for some other psychologist.*

Not far from where she was finishing up a session, Calem was taking another long walk to see his friend. He hesitated to call her his therapist because this relationship was different than that of a therapist and patient. In his mind a therapist was someone you didn't know, someone who only saw you once a week, someone who wasn't invested in your life or work the way Cordelia was invested in his. She genuinely cared about him, she wanted him to be okay, and he was aware of all that. The truth was that he didn't even like thinking of her as a friend.

"Friend" had become so ubiquitous and generic in today's society, the kid who used to sit next to you at lunch in the third grade, who you hadn't seen in decades, was now likely to be your "friend" on social media. In fact, it seemed like every person you met in person or online now instantly became a friend when you referenced to them in a story to one of your actual friends. No, Cordelia wasn't a friend in that way. In fact, the more time he spent around her, the less he wanted her as a friend or a therapist, and the more he wanted her in the way she wanted him.

As messed up as his head was over everything, he still had a sense of clarity and responsibility that was very well developed; he realized that even if he told Cordelia how he felt and asked her out that he'd probably make a shit boyfriend right now. After all, he was busier than ever, still not a hundred percent over his depression issues even if Tori was becoming more and more of a distant memory, and he spent most of his free time rolling around on the floor with other guys. But still, even with that measured and objective analysis of his emotional state, he still wanted her, and he still thought he might just do something about it.

Fuck therapy, he thought. *Fuck therapy, and fuck sitting on that couch and crying. I heard her last time, I know this latest victim isn't my fault, and I'm going to work furiously to catch this bastard. I know she's expecting me to go in there and be a fucking wreck, but that's not why I'm here.* He rang the bell to her place and mustered all of the courage he had inside of him. When she came to the door she looked amazing, more so than usual, and he didn't know why. There was a glimmer in her eyes, and an expression of compassion that was the most attractive thing he had ever seen.

"Hey," she said softly.

"Hey. Listen, I have an idea and instead of listening to my problems and giving me sound therapeutic advice afterwards, I just want you to say 'yes,' okay?"

"I'm listening."

"Let's get dinner," he said, enjoying the look of surprise on her face and the smile she was fighting. "I know a place."

CHAPTER FOURTEEN

"A food cart?" Cordelia asked, barely containing how snobbish it sounded. She had envisioned a restaurant—maybe at one of their usual places—but what she got instead was a Mexican food cart with a line halfway around the block.

"Street food is one of the best things this city has to offer. Do you trust me?" She nodded.

"You know I do."

"Then trust me now, it won't disappoint." The smell of the freshly prepared food was wafting through the summer air, and Cordelia breathed it in as deeply as her lungs would allow, taking in every individual spice she could identify, and a few that she couldn't. "I have to admit, that smells amazing, this might turn out to be the best dinner I've had in months."

"Angel will make sure of that," Calem answered. "He and his wife make the most authentic Mexican food around."

"You're on a first name basis with your food cart guy, huh? You must come here a lot."

"No, it's my first time, actually. I'm just really good at guessing people's names." The sarcasm was pouring out, and he managed to deliver that line with a straight face. It was Cordelia who cracked up.

"Asshole."

"A little bit, yeah," he said, smiling. "But you kind of walked into it."

"I kind of did, yeah. I think it's sweet, though."

"Me being a sarcastic asshole?"

"No, dummy. I mean a husband and wife cooking together, every day. There's something beautiful in that. I don't know, I'm sappy like that. Most people see people making their food, but I see romance when I look at that cart."

"I thought the same thing when I first met them. I still do."

"Really?" Cordelia asked, a little shocked at Calem's newly expressed sentimentally.

"Yeah," he said, looking right into Cordelia's eyes. "The idea of waking up with your significant other and having a common love, a common purpose, it's . . . I don't know, it seems like something to aspire to." Cordelia loved that, and, despite the mini-drama of how their last session had ended, there was something near perfect about how the evening was going. It was Manhattan, so there was always a large amount of people just about anywhere you went, but in certain settings that was ideal. The line of families and couples, paired with the amazing scents of great food and an ever-romantic Calem Walters made Cordelia feel happy that she accepted his invitation. It had been an unexpected invitation, but sometimes those were the best ones.

"The psychological literature proves what we're saying."

"What's that?"

"That spouses that cook and eat together have lower divorce rates and are generally healthier."

"The psychological literature?" Calem repeated, grinning at her. "I think you might be the only person in the history of food cart lines to cite peer reviewed academic journals while waiting for a taco on the street."

Cordelia smiled. She was cerebral, to say the least, and she wasn't used to having it appreciated by a guy. "Thank you?" she asked, not quite sure if she was being complimented or made fun of, or a little of both.

"Yes, it was a compliment," he answered, seeing her confusion at how to take his observation.

"And the history of food cart lines?" she joked, taking her chance at revenge. "You should write historical fiction for your next book. Granted, the history of food cart lines doesn't give you a lot of source material to work with." They laughed flirtatiously at each other's quips, a little harder than one should laugh at things that were only mildly funny, but that's what you did when you met someone new.

After a few more minutes of flirting and a few more steps closer to eating that amazing food, Cordelia realized something was changing between them. They'd gone out for food a million times, but never like this. He never asked her out like he did at her doorstop, and there was a decidedly romantic and flirty feel to the whole encounter. Rather than fight it, they both decided to just go with it.

The long line gave them more time to talk, and talk they did. It wasn't two colleagues discussing a case, or a patient and a doctor discussing psychological issues. It wasn't even two friends grabbing food because they had nothing better to do. This was a date, even though calling it that was the furthest thing from either of their minds. It felt so natural that it didn't need to be defined, and they just laughed and enjoyed each other's company while enjoying some of the best food the city had to offer.

She was feeling it tonight, and so was he. It was a meal; nothing extraordinary, and nothing that either of them was willing to classify as a date, but it signified something real; a turning point that each felt yet neither could fully explain to themselves. Sometimes it didn't take a dramatic event to break down the walls that we put up to protect ourselves; sometimes, as they both now realized, it just took action. In this case, some to-die-for Mexican food and the type of conversation that reminded them how much they meant to each other. It was ironic that each of them had been individually torturing themselves over their feelings toward one another. Each of them understood the complexities of their situation, but they still knew that their feelings for one another were undeniable, and it was a fight they were both slowly submitting to without the other knowing.

They walked around the city for a few minutes after they ate. It was another beautiful Manhattan night, and they were taking full advantage of it. This part of the city wasn't filled with tourists pointing their cameras up in the air at all buildings; and it wasn't too swarmed with people. It was quiet; intimate; the kind of setting that allowed for a walk to do what hours of conversation could never quite achieve. That's why, when he felt it was right, Calem reached down and grabbed Cordelia's hand. And, to his surprise, she gripped it more tightly than he had. It was another small gesture, yet it signified so much more than it seemed to. He looked into her eyes as they stopped walking, and each of them knew what was coming next. Forgetting his doubts and silencing his anxieties, he leaned in and kissed her gently, and she reciprocated. "Calem, I . . ."

But before she could finish he kissed her again, this time for longer, and she let herself get completely swept up in the moment. He reached up and gripped her face, holding it lightly as he continued to kiss her passionately. It seemed to go on for an eternity. When their faces separated each one treated the moment like it was meant to happen, and maybe it was. There was no long conversation about what the kiss meant, and there sure as hell was no expression of regret. There was only them, the gorgeous night sky above them, and a burning desire for more. He gripped her hand again and they kept walking with no words, as though nothing had happened, yet their entire world had just shifted. After a few minutes her house stood before them, as did a choice neither wanted to admit.

Cordelia understood what inviting him in meant. She knew that it wouldn't be for a post-dinner drink, or to "see the rest of the place," or any other bullshit pretense. She knew that the real invitation was for them to experience each other in the way each of them wanted most deeply. Things had changed, suddenly, and each was ready to see how far it would go. They knew it before tonight; they each felt the attraction between them for some time, yet they fought themselves out of a sense of guilt or professionalism. Now it was time for all of that to come to an end.

She didn't understand how anything prior to that moment had

transpired to lead them there, staring into each other's eyes with a deep, mutual desire, but none of that mattered. It was real, and they both felt it. It was just up to her to make the final move; the decision about what happened next was entirely up to her. "Do you want to come in?" she asked. He nodded quickly, as though anticipating the question before she asked it, and a few seconds later they were inside her home. "Can I get you a—" Calem didn't waste any time, cutting off her words and kissing her passionately, only this kiss was different than the one on the street a few minutes ago.

He kissed her in a way that let her know that it was only the beginning of the experience she was about to have. His lips were soft, but they pressed firmly against hers, causing a tingle that shot down from her mouth down deep to between her legs. And it was there that she really needed Calem; there in the throbbing wetness that began to soak her underwear in anticipation of his touch. She didn't have to wait long. His hands began on her face, but they didn't linger there for long, drifting slowly down and cupping her waist, pulling her whole body into him. "Cordy," he said to her. "You're so fucking hot."

She would never have pulled away, but even if she wanted to there was no escaping the strength of his grip. He was a mountain next to her; a body meant to be touched and lost within, and as soon as she crashed against him she could feel his excitement pressing against her hip. His body was speaking to her in a perfect articulation that his words could never express. Its urgency whispered to her. No bed, no shower, no living room couch; right here where we stand. She complied with her eyes, and he lifted her and walked them into her office. He hoisted her up onto the edge of her desk; he could barely contain his throbbing erection.

She leaned back for a second to undo the buttons on her shirt, but she didn't make it past the second one before Calem ripped the whole thing open, pulling at each side with his hands and sending her buttons flying across the floor. It was the hottest thing she had ever experienced, and it only made her anticipate what was going to happen even more. He pulled her back where she belonged, forward toward him, so that her ass balanced just on the edge of the desk. After he pulled her shirt completely off she wrapped her legs around him to balance. Next was her bra, he reached around her back to unclasp the black lace, and as he did she leaned in and sucked his neck as hard as she could. The suction felt amazing, and he knew it was time to return the favor.

As her bra fell to the ground her erect nipples pointed right at him, perfectly centered on her soft breasts, and begging for his mouth. He leaned forward and circled his tongue around her left nipple as a tease, feeling its firmness contrast with the soft pressure of his tongue. Done teasing, he put his mouth around it, sucking hard and causing her to scream out; she was sensitive, and she felt her whole body jolt as the suction of his mouth closed in around her. And just as soon as it had begun, his mouth was gone. After all, it had other work to do. As he reached his right hand down between her legs . . .

Cordelia

. . . I think I'm gonna come right now. I'm the most turned on I have ever been in my life, as the throbbing ache between my legs was met with the strength of his fingers. First, they danced on the outside of my pussy, teasing me uncontrollably, moving up and down on the outside of my lips, just barely touching my clit. He knows what he's doing, and he moves with confidence. "Don't stop," I whisper as his hand leaves "Please don't stop." He has me begging him, and he's rewarding my submission with the talent of his fingers. He thrusts his hand back between my legs and starts rubbing my clit in powerful circular motions. I'm dripping wet, and I know that I'm soaking his hands, but the wetter I get, the more his fingers move me closer and closer to orgasm. With his free hand he reaches behind me and pulls my head back forcefully by my hair. I don't fight him, allowing my head to fall to the side as he buries his lips in my exposed neck, all the while his fingers reaching deeper and deeper inside me.

His erection is bursting out of his pants, straining to get loose, and I can feel its frustration as it jabs against my leg. Just when I think I'm about to come he slows his fingers and puts both hands under my ass to pull my underwear down. I lift up for a second and that's all he needed. I'm exposed, spread eagle on my desk, and I can't believe how badly I want him. "Take me upstairs," I say to him. "Take me to my bed." But he doesn't listen.

"No," he answers. "I'm going to fuck you right here on your desk." His control is so fucking hot that I can't do anything but follow his command, and I'm willing to give up all control to let this beautiful man have me in any way he wants me. "Now lay down." His command is mine to follow, and I oblige him willingly, putting my back across my desk as I hear him undo the buckle of his belt. Its jingle makes the anticipation of what's about to happen even greater, and my body goes stiff.

"Fuck me, Calem," I yell, and once again he ignores my wish.

"No," he says. "Not yet." He drops to his knees, lowering his mouth to rest between my legs. He starts by kissing my inner thighs, working his tongue from the inside of my knees all the way up to my wet pussy. My underwear is gone, and there's nothing stopping his tongue from making me feel pure ecstasy. My legs shake as he gets closer and closer, working his way upward until I feel his warm lips on mine. I grip his hair in my fingers and he sucks on my clit with the perfect amount of pressure to drive me to the brink of orgasm again, his finger thrusting in and out of me while his mouth works its magic. Oh God, I'm so turned on!

When he pulls his mouth away I arch my back, shooting my hips upwards to ask for more of the pleasure that he's bringing me. I won't have to wait long. I feel his hands on both of my hips, pulling me toward him, but instead of scooting my butt closer to him I sit up and jump off the table. His cock's exposed, hard as a rock, and begging for my mouth, so I drop to my knees in front of my desk. He moans deeply as I take his head into the suction of my lips, forming a seal from which there was no escape. I hold on to his shaft with my hand and as I guide him deeper into my mouth we make the most intense eye contact. I can feel his body tense up the second I look at him, and he can't hold back the sounds of ecstasy coming from his throat.

Calem

I'm about to come, so I pull her back and she jumps to her feet. I've never gotten head like she's giving me; she knows how to use her mouth and her hand in perfect unison, and I'm so turned on that I need to stop before I lose it completely. Once she's on her feet we start to make out again, her hand reaching down and stroking me as fast as she can. I don't want to wait another second. As I pull out a condom from my wallet she puts herself back on the edge of the desk and lays back submissively, inviting me inside of her. Her hair's loose from me pulling at it, and it falls long and messed up behind her head, bringing out the blue of her eyes and turning me on even more. She's so beautiful that I actually take a minute to just look at her; her face red and flushed, her eyes burning with desire, her perfect breasts moving up and down as she tries to fill her lungs with air. "You're so fucking hot, Cordelia," I say, looking deep in her eyes.

"I want you inside me, Calem," she answers. "Don't make me wait any longer."

"No more waiting," I say, my cock throbbing in my hand waiting to slide inside of her. But instead I decide to surprise her. I let go of myself and put my hands under her ass and pull her toward me. When she's closer I reach behind her back and pull her upright. Her hair's a mess, and she's breathing like she's just finished running a marathon. She looks so fucking hot, and it takes all the control I have to not take her right then and there.

I lift her up like a feather, and she wraps her legs around me like a vice, I only needed to take a few steps before she's . . .

Cordelia

. . . slammed up against the wall. I yell out of surprise without even realizing. It's fucking hot that he's taking control of me, and as I'm pinned up against the wall, unable to move anything except my legs, my pussy is screaming for him. I try to struggle but it's useless; he has complete control of my body, and his dick is like a steel rod shooting into my leg. "Fuck me," I yell, and he holds me against the wall with one hand, and with the other he reaches down and positions himself to slide right into me. When he does I can't help but yell out. He's big, really fucking big, and I feel the breadth of him fill me with a kind of tightness that I've never experienced before. My legs are tight around his hips, and he pulls me away from the wall slightly and holds onto my ass. I feel weightless as he slams my whole body into his, suspending me in mid-air and thrusting his cock into me as he pulls my small body in and out.

He feels strong enough to hold me there forever, but I whisper in his ear, "Take me upstairs." He thrusts in and out of me with a few more powerful slams of our bodies before cradling me in his huge arms and walking me to my bedroom. Once inside he places me gently on the bed, and as I lie back he grabs each of my ankles, and pulls my legs to opposite sides of the room. As soon as the back of my head hits the bed I'm filled up again, the wetness of my pussy letting him glide into me without any effort, and before I know it . . .

Calem

Her tits are bouncing around as I shake her body with my thrusts, and I almost don't know where to look as I fuck her. No matter where my eyes go there's something exciting me more and more. In her beautiful eyes I see a desire that makes me never want to stop. I look between us and I see my cock going in and out of her pussy, which is so wet that I have trouble not slipping out completely. I don't want to come too fast, but the feeling of her pussy constricting me is bringing me closer with each passing second. I slow down to hold off from coming.

"What's the matter?" she asks, out of breath.

"Nothing," I reassure her. "I just needed to slow down. I don't want to this end just yet."

She doesn't say anything at all in response except, "Go to my top drawer." Beyond intrigued, I leave her soaking wet and throbbing on the bed, and I make my way around to her nightstand. Inside the top drawer, I see it. I knew exactly what it was, but I've never seen one quite like it before . . .

Cordelia

My vibrator is calling for him. And not just any vibrator, my special-order clit stimulator in a custom purple color. Most guys are intimidated by it, but next to Calem's dick it looks like a purple toothpick, and he has the confidence to know how to use it without feeling inadequate. He takes it out and holds it up, teasing me with a smile. I smile back, looking from his eyes down to the rock-hard dick staring at me, sad that it's no longer inside of me where it belongs. "Is this what you want?" he asks, knowing full well that it's exactly what I want. "Well?" he asks again.

"You know it is," I say.

"I want you to ask me for it."

Oh my God, I'm so fucking wet! I'll do anything that he asks me right now, even if that means begging. "Give it to me now, Calem." In a second he's on me, the buzzing sound an indicator of the pleasure we're both about to receive. He stands over me as my legs are spread-eagle and my knees are pointed up toward the ceiling. He walks between them and starts with the vibrator. Slowly lowering it down toward my pussy, the buzzing gets louder and louder until I feel the stimulation. My eyes roll to the back of my head and I lie down to let myself feel all the pleasure at once. A few seconds later I feel him in me, pulling in and out; slowly at first, then faster, then slowly again. I know that he's . . .

Calem

. . . Trying to switch up my movements with the speed of her vibrator. She feels so tight that I'm enjoying going as slow as I can, letting her feel every inch of me go deeper and deeper into her, until our hip bones are pressed against one another, and there's nowhere to go but back out again. All the while I'm holding the vibrator against her clit, and moving it around, slowly, watching her reaction as I do. I can tell that she's close, and if I wasn't wearing a condom I would have come myself by now. She tells me that she's about to come, and I feel the contractions of her pussy around me, which brings me even closer. I know that we're about to finish at the same time, and I hold on as long as I can until I see her scream and gyrate in a way that lets me know exactly what's happening. As she writhes on the bed I let go, and my orgasm is powerful, my cum shooting out of me as she arches her back and screams. A few seconds later we're both done, and we . . .

Collapsed on each other in total exhaustion. In a few hours they had gone from friends to lovers, and their first time did not disappoint. Calem lay next her; their sweaty bodies glistening in the afterglow of their lovemaking, and the sounds of their heavy breathing filling the empty space. "That was . . ."

"Incredible," she said, finishing his thought. The two lay there for a few minutes, naked as the day they were born, and satisfied in a way neither had ever been before. The shift had started and ended in the same place, with him asking her to dinner, and she accepting. Now they were here as lovers, and after a few minutes they curled up under her fancy covers and drifted off to sleep in each other's arms.

CHAPTER FIFTEEN

She slept so well that it hurt to wake up. She shut her eyes again and curled the sheets around her neck, trying to deny the daylight that was creeping in through her bedroom window, threatening to rob her of any more rest. *Five more minutes, Mom, then I'll get ready for school, okay?* What finally got her up wasn't the sun, and it wasn't some sense of being a productive citizen. What finally forced her eyes to accept the daytime was Calem missing from the bed. She rolled her body over to the left side, expecting to bump into him and possibly be a little spoon for a few stolen minutes. Instead, she almost rolled right off the bed, and had to put her hand out to grab the edge. *Where is he?*

Sitting up and rubbing the night out of her eyes, she stretched her arms over her head, still naked, and looked around the room. Maybe he was in the shower, or downstairs making himself a weak cup of coffee with her Keurig. But none of those things seemed to be what was actually happening; just a continuation of the dream she might have been having a few minutes before. In reality her place was empty. No Calem and no Haddie. She knew that without looking because her houseguest was loud in the morning, usually doing yoga in the living room, making coffee, or talking on the phone. But what struck

Cordelia most was the silence. *Where the hell did he go?* she wondered.

Still looking around the room for some sign of life other than hers, she noticed a white piece of paper on her nightstand that was held down by a pen she kept in her room. It read,

No, I didn't freak out and run away, I have to get a training session in and work on the case. I'll be at the gym till nine, then at the station. I need your eyes on this to help prevent another victim, so if you don't have patients meet me at one of those places. P.S. Last night was amazing.

Everything in the middle of the note was filler to her eyes; not really, she was invested in helping catch the rapist, but in an immediate sense it was the first and last lines that she was most concerned with. She assumed that something with work had taken him out of her bed after that amazing night they had, but the insecure part of her thought that he had a terrible time and had snuck out like it was a regrettable one-night stand. Sometimes even the most confident and successful of people could suffer insecurities like that, but Calem's note had quieted that devil whispering in her ear.

She checked her phone. There was still enough time to make herself presentable, grab a quick coffee, food would have to be a later on in the day thing, and meet him for the tail end of his workout. If she missed him she could just go right to the station, but it didn't seem like a problem. As she was getting ready she reflected on the past twelve hours between her and Calem. Last night was the fulfillment of some of her deepest fantasies; the explosion at the end of a long-burned wick, and he hadn't disappointed in the bedroom. There was an expectation of guilt, or complicated emotions, but all she felt that morning was pure bliss, the lingering happiness from everything that had taken place the day before. And, for once, she just embraced the happy feeling without analyzing everything to death. It felt nice, and she deserved to feel nice.

It took longer than she thought to get out of the house, so she decided to skip the gym and head right to the station to meet Calem and Jesse. Haddie was still out God-knew-where when Cordelia locked up, so she texted her real quick just to make sure she was alive. It was a much hotter day outside than it had been yesterday. New York summers could be erratic like that. One day it could practically feel like fall, with cool breezes and overcast skies that threatened rain and then there were days like this that seemed cartoonishly hot and humid. The ones where the ice cream truck owners became wealthy on the lines of kids waiting for that vanilla cone with rainbow sprinkles; and where the fire department had to be called to shut off the hydrants that tenants had found a way to turn on so their children could cool off in the street.

Walking seemed like a terrible idea, and Cordelia knew she'd be drenched in sweat by the time she walked through the station doors, so she called an Uber on her app and decided that traffic was preferable to losing half her body weight in fluids. Twenty minutes later she was there. Jesse was just arriving and greeted her with a big hug. "Hey, we have you today?" he asked.

"You have me any day you need me, but yeah, Calem asked me to look over some of the new evidence from the other night."

"Yeah, that was a good idea," he said somberly. "This whole case is a fuckin' mess, off the record."

"What do you mean a mess?"

"We're doing all the right things, like we always do. And not to sound arrogant, but between the two of us and you, we have enough brain power to solve the Kennedy assassination, so it doesn't make sense that we're not much further along than we were after the first victim. This fucker is good. I hate to say it, but he's not some out of control crackpot grabbing women in an alley and leaving evidence everywhere. He knows how to cover his tracks."

"We'll get him, Jess. It's just that progress in these situations has to be measured contextually; we can't expect a movie ending to this one. It might have to be a grind."

"It already is a grind, Cordelia, and it's us who are getting the worst of it."

"Well then, don't get discouraged, and do your best to ignore the pressure I know you're getting from your bosses."

"Easier said than done," he said. "But I know what you mean, it's good advice. It isn't just pressure from One Police Plaza or a sense of failure that's hurting us."

"What else?" Cordelia asked.

"This is weird to talk about standing outside my precinct in the middle of the street . . ."

"Oh, I'm sorry, did you want to go somewhere else?"

"There's a deli across the street there, have you had coffee yet?"

"Yeah, but more caffeine is never a bad thing. Take me there and let's talk."

"I hear that," Jesse agreed. "Come with me, we can talk over there where there are less ears."

Cordelia was intrigued by whatever it was Jesse wanted to talk about. She didn't know him that well; at least not on a personal level that extended past an acquaintance, and she'd never really spoken to him without Calem around, so she was curious where her serendipitous meeting on the way into the station was going to lead. He looked tense, not his usual light-hearted self, and her immediate impulse was to go into therapist mode. They got their coffees and sat down at a little table next to the windows that looked out on the station. "So, tell me, what is it about this case that has you guys so frustrated."

"I can't speak for Calem, but for me it's personal," Jesse said. "I don't know if civilians can understand this sort of thing, but some cases hit very close to home, if you know what I mean, and not always the ones you think."

"Like what?" she asked.

"People think the most horrific crimes are the ones that stick with you, the gruesome murders and things like that. But the ones that really get inside of you and keep you up at night are the ones you have some emotional investment in. They try to train us to be objective, and mostly we just get used to horrible things, but in some cases—"

Cordelia interrupted because she could see he was getting a little emotional, and she wanted to give him a break from having to talk. "Listen, if it's any consolation, even though I'm a civilian, like you said, I can still relate to what you're talking about. Our jobs are similar,

Jess, whether you think of it like that or not. I don't have to catch people like you do, but I do just as much problem solving and hearing about cases as you do, maybe more so. And psychologists are also told to be objective, to not let yourself get pulled into other people's dramas and illnesses, but it's hard sometimes, I get it. What is it about this one, though?"

Jesse wasn't making eye contact when it was his turn to speak; he just looked out the window like he was lost in thought, the emotion still evident in his voice. "I don't wanna speak for my partner . . ."

"We already spoke about it; I know what's going on with him. I'm asking about you. You're fifty percent of that partnership, so I want to know what your issues are." Cordelia was talking to him like a patient. She knew Jesse wasn't the type of guy who was going to come into a formal therapy session and bare his soul on her couch, so she took this random opportunity the universe (or Manhattan traffic) granted her to help out the case in a different sort of way.

"I have a big family," he started, looking out the window again, as though looking Cordelia in the eyes might be too much for him. "Irish mom, Italian dad—you know, typical New York cop. Dad was on the force for thirty years. Anyhow, I have five siblings; three sisters and two brothers."

"Your mom must be a strong woman," Cordelia joked.

"She is, yeah. So, my youngest sister, Emily, is a junior in college right now. Last year, in her second semester as a sophomore, she was raped at a frat party."

"Oh my God," Cordelia said, instinctively putting her hand over his as a sign of comfort. "That's horrible. What happened?"

"One of those typical stories you hear; a party with too much alcohol, drunk assholes looking to get laid, young girls who haven't been prepared to protect themselves against sexual predators who don't look like sexual predators. The whole nine."

"Was the guy arrested?"

"Of course not. Do you know how hard it is to convict a rapist that's obviously a rapist, let alone a he said/she said case where the victim was there voluntarily, and drunk? Easier to hit a homerun out of

Yankee Stadium. The school basically blamed my sister, didn't believe her story, and declined to do anything to that piece of shit. She had to transfer schools, obviously, and spent over a year in therapy trying to move on."

"I'm so sorry that happened," she said, her hand still over his. "This world is a fucked up place. But you don't need to hear that from me to know it's true. How is she doing now?"

"Much better, luckily, but it's been rough. She still has some bad days where she suffers from depression and anxiety. And she hasn't dated anyone since that happened. Can you imagine that? Young girl goes off to college, wanting to experience the world for the first time, and she runs into some scumbag looking to ruin all of that. I gotta stop talking about this; I'm going to get angry. I'm already fuckin' angry."

"I understand, you have every right to be angry, and so does Emily, but she's done all the right things. She sounds like a fighter."

"Yeah, she's a champion. I'm proud of how she handled that situation."

"Think about what fighting is, Jess. I know you train with Calem, right?"

"Yeah," he answered.

"When you roll in jujitsu, or spar with your striking, the goal isn't to never get hit. That would be unrealistic. The goal is to learn how to take the hits, and keep moving forward. That's what being a fighter is, and your sister is going to be fine. You have to let that go as you investigate. You both have to let the emotion go."

Jesse nodded and listened, making eye contact whenever Cordelia was talking to him. He was an interesting man; younger, emotional, in need of attention and glory, but good at his core. It was clear that he came from a good family and only wanted the best for people. He was a good man and a good cop, this case was just kicking his ass. "Thanks for listening, do I need to pay you or something, I don't know how this whole therapy thing works."

"I think the coffee you bought me will cover it." She smiled at him and he smiled back. He was still stressed, and so was Calem, and no quick deli conversation would take all of that away, but he needed to uncork the bottle a little, and just say the words that had been bothering him since this case started. Sometimes that was enough to kick you in the ass and help you move forward. "And thanks for confiding in me, everything you told me stays between us, no matter what."

"Thanks, Cordelia, you're the best."

"I know," she joked. "And, oh, while I have you here, I know how you can pay me back for our little session."

"How's that?"

"Stop with the corny pickup lines if you and Haddie are ever in the same room again, that shit was killing me at McNulty's. Really bad, Jess."

"I don't know what the hell that was," he said, his normal self coming back to the forefront. "I didn't even recognize myself, I was saying all kinds of dumb shit like I had never spoken to a pretty girl before. She just had a weird effect on me, I don't know why. I hope I didn't blow it."

"Haddie's not like that. She's beautiful, for sure, but she isn't that girl. She found it cute, actually, but don't tell her I told you that."

"Oh yeah?" Jesse seemed invigorated by those words, as though he was getting a second chance at a girl he liked, and Cordelia was psyched to see the change in his mood from almost crying a few minutes ago to looking like he could conquer the world. "Maybe put in a good word for me, huh?"

"I would if I knew where the fuck she was. She stayed out last night. I think she's loving being back in the city. But I'm sure we'll talk later on."

Calem was pounding the pavement inside the station. He looked intense to outside observers, like he always did, but inside he was still warm from last night. He could compartmentalize like that; allowing himself a totally selfish feeling of bliss, and then getting right back to trying to find a criminal he was going after. That kind of shift threw people off sometimes, but Calem found it useful for balancing work and non-work aspects of his life. He hated having to run out like he did, and he considered waking her up and saying something before he left, but he didn't want to interrupt her sleep. She looked so beautiful with the side of her face pressed gently against the pillow, and her hair framing her shoulders. He wasn't about to mess up that image by waking her, so instead he left a note telling her where he'd be, and how much he enjoyed himself.

He was expecting her soon, so he took a break from the horrors of the crime to think back. He wasn't usually the most introspective of people when it came to personal things, but his time with Cordelia was changing his outlook on things. He was still the intense, gruff, nose-to-the-grindstone cop, but he was learning how to deal with his own demons, and how to grow as a human being, and it was all because of her. A year ago; hell, even a few months ago, the idea that he would be spending the night with Cordelia Summers, and that he'd be developing some intense feelings toward her was unthinkable, something he would have laughed off. But now he realized that it wasn't some spontaneous attraction that came out of nowhere, he had always felt some type of way toward her, the only difference was now he was allowing himself to recognize those feelings, and there was no going back.

When she and Jesse walked into the station, Calem didn't even notice his own partner. All he saw was her, and the whole room seemed to slowly fade into oblivion, until there was nothing left but her stride toward his desk, and the beauty of her eyes to look into. Of course Jesse snapped him right out of that. "I found this one outside."

"And you didn't think to get me a coffee. What kind of partner are you?"

"A selfish, yet well-caffeinated one. I'm sorry, man, you want me to go back and grab one?"

"Nah, I'm okay," Calem said. "I'll grab one later on. There's work to do now. Why don't we work in the backroom, there's a table there and we can spread out a little. Jesse, can you go open it up and grab one of these boxes of evidence?"

"You got it."

When Jesse was gone, Calem, in a very un-Calem like moment, pulled Cordelia close to him and kissed her on the mouth in front of everyone. It shocked her, but that didn't stop her from kissing him right back. People in the room were looking, but he didn't give a damn and neither did she. "Well that was . . . unexpected."

"This has all been unexpected for me. In the best way possible. But enough of that," he said, returning to his normal self. "We have to catch this fucker."

CHAPTER SIXTEEN

Like a scene from a bad movie, where the main character drops something breakable, and always in slo-mo during the shocking reveal, Cordelia found her coffee on the floor when she realized what she was looking at. It was like that, only the shock was real; a genuine surprise of the worst kind that hit Cordelia like a punch to the jaw, as though she had no control over her motor skills.

Sophia Hernandez was the living embodiment of New York. The thirty-year-old daughter of immigrants from Ecuador and Columbia, Sophia was working nights to finish a degree in radiology so that she could work more hours to support her son, Carlo. Sophia grew up in Brooklyn, moving to Manhattan to finish up school and forge a better life for herself after her son's father left her high and dry. Twice a week Carlo slept over his grandparent's place back in Brooklyn so his mom could go to night classes. She was in her last year, and happy that an end was finally in sight. She was late for her class over some drama with her ex who refused to keep up with his childcare payments, and the phone call had delayed her leaving on time. She was angry, flustered, and emotional when the doorbell rang.

Sophia was a smart New Yorker, which meant that she was conditioned to be aware of danger; of things that could hurt you. All parents taught their kids to be safe; to be aware, but parents of city kids most of all. The geography begged for a heightened sense of awareness than did the white picket fences of suburbia, and Sophia considered herself on the smarter side of keeping herself safe. When the bell rang, she wiped the tears from her face and tried to compose herself. She was expecting a diaper delivery from Amazon, and she didn't want to look like a crazy woman, not even to the delivery guy, so she opened the door without hesitation.

When she woke up all she heard was the sobs from her parents, who were standing over her hospital bed, and she could see out of only one eye, the other having been closed from repeated blows to the face with a blunt object. The police suspected a lamp, but they were still investigating. The silver lining was that she didn't remember any of it, and at that stage it was a blessing that she was still alive. Doctors were running a rape kit for fluids. Sophia was everything the rapist's MO demanded: she was young, she was different than all of the other victims, and at the time of her attack she was alone in broad daylight.

She was also one of Cordelia's patients.

When the coffee cup hit the floor Calem ran over to her immediately with his hands outstretched, worried that something was wrong with her physically. "Are you all right?" When she didn't answer Calem got concerned. He knew it wasn't physical right away, even though she wasn't moving. "What is it?"

"I know her," Cordelia answered, the tears welling up in her eyes. "She's one of mine."

"A patient?" Jesse asked. Cordelia didn't have the words, she just nodded her head in affirmation, her eyes never leaving those disturbing pictures.

"Jesse, can you get someone to clean this up?"

"Yeah, of course."

"I'm sorry," she said, barely able to hold the tears back. "I didn't realize I dropped it."

"Forget all that, it doesn't matter. I'm sorry you had to see all of this. How well do you know the victim?"

The victim. That's what happened when something like this

happened, you went from being a human being to the holder of a title you could never shake.

Sophia, the rape victim.

Sophia the survivor of an attack.

Sophia, the woman recovering from a brutal assault.

Sophia Hernandez, patient of Dr. Cordelia Summers.

"I knew her very well, but I can't divulge any of what I saw her for. But she's a very strong woman."

"I'm sure she is." It was all Calem could offer. There was no sugarcoating what had happened to Sophia; it was all there in lurid detail and photos that left little to the imagination. At least she was alive, that was something. Had he known that Cordelia knew the victim, he never would have asked her for help that day, and he found it a really odd coincidence that there was a connection between them.

"My motivation to catch this bastard just went through the roof."

"I'm already there," Calem added. "But I have to give you your own advice right now. I know it's easier said than done, but you have to put your emotions aside, remember? If you want to help Sophia, the best thing we can do is just get to work."

"Then let's stop talking and get to it."

"Yes, ma'am."

Three hours was a long time to look at all the crime scene materials, but they had done some good work together by the time they were finished. Cordelia was trying to keep it together about Sophia, but it was hard. It was one thing to hear about an "unidentified victim" that has no name and no face, but it was quite another to know the person who got attacked personally. She couldn't tell any of this to Calem or Jesse, but Sophia was seeing her for major depression that surrounded all the stress with her ex, but she was working through it for the betterment of her son. She was a model patient, and someone who Cordelia liked personally very much. The three hours at the station had worked to calm her nerves after the initial shock, and now the horror she felt when she first saw who the latest victim was, was replaced by the strongest sense of motivation she had ever felt to catch the man responsible.

Then there was the Calem thing.

Before leaving the station she had asked him and Jesse over to hang out at her place later on when they were done with work. She assumed Haddie would be back from whatever adventures she had been on the night before, and that they would be a foursome. It struck Cordelia on the way home that she was treating them like they were on a double date or something, when in reality neither of them was officially a couple. Sure, she had slept with Calem and they both felt something very strong for each other, but they hadn't shared a word between them since that didn't involve the case. And as far as Jesse and Haddie went, that wasn't a thing yet either, and if the last time was a prologue, it never would be. *Stop it, you're over analyzing, it's just hanging out at your house with people you care about, normal people do this all the time, stop thinking everything to death.*

She could see Haddie from the cab window. She was on the steps talking to someone else in typical fashion, but Cordelia couldn't see who. After paying the guy and getting out she yelled to her friend, "Thanks for returning my text this morning; I thought you were lying in a ditch somewhere."

"I'm good, Mom," Haddie joked, turning around to face her mothering friend. Cordelia thought about waking up this morning; how comfortable she felt in bed, how full of happiness she was, and how reluctant she was to end that with the reality of the day. Had she known it would be a day of shocking events, she might have never gotten up.

When Haddie turned to speak, Cordelia could see the other person on her stoop. It was Johnathan Kenenna—the crackpot patient who hadn't been heard from since storming out while shouting profanity at her. *What the hell is he doing here?* she asked herself. *We don't have a session.* Cordelia literally ignored Haddie's attempts at humor and looked right at Johnathan, who was already staring back. "What are you doing here?" she asked.

"Jeez, is that anyway to greet your friend," Haddie joked, but Cordelia wasn't having any of it. She looked right past Haddie and asked for a second time, only this time Haddie interrupted. "Hello? Cord, if you'd look at me for a sec I'd explain. This is Marvin. I met him last night and he was nice enough to wait with me because I lost the spare house key you gave me." *Marvin? Who the hell is Marvin?*

"Go inside."

"What," Haddie asked, shocked by Cordelia's tone.

"Go. Inside. Now." It didn't take a third ask. She gave Haddie her keys without even looking at her, and kept the intense stare with Johnathan (or Marvin) the entire time. Once Haddie was inside and the front door was closed she confronted this lunatic. "What the fuck is going on here, Johnathan. Is Johnathan really your name?"

"It's one of them, sure. But there are others. I made Marvin up last night, but I sell it so well, don't I? Your friend bought it hook, line, and sinker. But I thought she might, she seems like the gullible type." Cordelia got a chill in her bones, the kind of feeling that was too primal to be explained scientifically; the type that indicated something was very wrong.

"Who the hell are you?"

"Look, I've gotta go, but I'm sure I'll be seeing you again soon, your friend seems to like me, so who knows." The man known to her as Johnathan started to walk away and she literally didn't know what to do. Technically he didn't do anything wrong, but he was freaking Cordelia out, and he clearly wasn't who she thought he was when he sat in her office.

"Wait," she yelled as he walked away, not quite knowing what else to do. As he stepped into a cab parked a few feet away he turned and looked Cordelia in the eyes.

"Oh, I meant to ask you, did you ever get that Amazon package you were waiting for?"

"What?"

He stepped in the cab and it pulled away before she had time to process what he just said. By the time she realized she didn't know what to do; she was stunned into silence, and if she had another cup of coffee to drop, the street in front of her place would have been flooded with dark roast.

She ran inside as fast as her legs could carry her; the anxiety pumping through her body and taking her breath away. "Haddie!" she yelled. It was an overreaction, as Haddie stepped out slowly from the kitchen looking alarmed.

"Yeah, so what the hell was all that? I know it's your place and all, and I know we didn't discuss me bringing people over, but you didn't have to—"

"Listen to me; I need you to tell me everything about how you met that guy, like right now."

"But I'm having a sandwich."

"Fuck your sandwich," Cordelia shouted. Her anxiety had gotten the better of her and she traded normal interaction for a sense of urgency. After seeing the incredulous expression on Haddie's face Cordelia took a moment to take a deep breath and bring it down a notch. "I'm sorry, I didn't mean to yell at you, but you don't understand who that was, and I need you to just accept my apology and answer me."

"Fine, apology accepted, and I met him last night at a bar near here I was hanging out at."

"You approached him?"

"No, actually, he came up to me."

"Did I come up in any way?"

"Jesus, Cordelia, not everything is about you."

"Please, Haddie," Cordelia pleaded. "Just believe for a second that I'm not being arrogant and answer me. Did I come up at all? Or my practice, or anything I was working on?"

"I might have said that I was staying with my friend, and I think I called you by your first name, but nothing about your job or any of the cop stuff. Why? What's going on?"

She couldn't' say for sure what was going on, but she was pretty sure that Johnathan had just confessed to her that he was the Manhattan rapist, and there was only one person she needed to call.

CHAPTER SEVENTEEN

No one in the room knew how to react, and Calem was doing his best to stay objective in the face of Cordelia's minor hysteria. She called him in a panic, insisting that he leave work and come over immediately, which he did without questioning why. He arrived to a worked-up Cordelia, who was practically interrogating Haddie when he walked in. The whole thing reminded him of a scene from his job, and Cordelia was playing the role of cop. *Tell me everything about last night? Did he ask about my address? Was he with anyone else? A thousand rapid-fire questions and a confused houseguest wondering what the hell was happening.*

"First off, are you both okay?" Calem asked

"Besides my generous host yelling at me and treating me like a child, yeah, I'm all good."

"Haddie, be quiet, there are more important things happening here than your comfort," said Cordelia. Haddie got that impression, but she still didn't like being spoken to like she was a kid, and she was getting tired of it.

"Well why don't you just include me in the discussion and stop freaking out and drilling me with questions. You're not a cop, Cordelia, you know, no matter how much you work with them. And the only actual cop in the room is much calmer than you are."

"That's because he didn't just meet the Manhattan rapist," Cordelia said bluntly.

"Cordelia, before we draw any conclusions I think you need to calm down and—"

"Don't tell me to calm down," she interrupted. The deep breathing did nothing to calm the anxiety she was still feeling. She felt helpless, like she had just let a dangerous person slip through her fingers, and all she could think about was getting him, she didn't care how rude she was coming across. Calem did his best to understand and not speak to her like a witness, but he wasn't used to seeing her so agitated.

"Cordelia, I understand that you're worked up, and I want to listen to everything you have to say right now, but I can't do that if you're yelling at everyone in the room. You called me. So, if you want me to listen I need you to take a step back and tell me everything that happened, calmly." He was looking right in her eyes and speaking in the quietest and most confident tone he had; he was avoiding his cop voice, and instead just trying to be there for her in a way that would slow her heart rate down.

"I'm sorry," she said. "To both of you. It's been a rough day, I apologize."

"It's okay," Haddie said. She came over and gave Cordelia a hug and rubbed her back in small gentle circles. "Just tell us what's going on."

The three of them sat down together in Cordelia's office, with Haddie and Calem on the couch and Cordelia in her chair, which she moved from around her desk so they were all sitting together. The mood was tense, but everyone was calm and listening to each other. Cordelia told them everything: about Johnathan—or Marvin— or whoever he was about what he said to her, and, most importantly, what he said to her before leaving. It was the last part Calem was most interested in. "He said Amazon? He specifically said that? You didn't mishear him?"

"He said Amazon," she answered. "And it's not only what he said to me, it's how he said it. It's hard to explain if you weren't there, but you have to trust me, he said that on purpose so I would catch on. He was grinning when he said it."

"But, wait," Haddie interrupted. "I don't get it."

"I'm going to take you into confidence by telling you this, Haddie, and I'm going to trust you won't say anything at all." Calem was serious about keeping confidential information confidential, but this was a weird circumstance.

"I promise," Haddie said.

"The latest victim was attacked by a man pretending to be a delivery man, and the reason she opened the door was that she was waiting for a diaper delivery from Amazon."

"Shit," Haddie said, looking at Cordelia and beginning to understand that she may have spent the previous evening with a serial rapist. "I can't believe I brought this guy here."

"You didn't know," Cordelia assured her. "And he was my patient for a little while, but now I have to question everything. His name, his previous therapy—everything. If he is who we think he might be, then he obviously wasn't coming in for therapy, so why did he come here? Was he stalking me? Trying to get information? Jesus, I let him leave on his own. He was walking through my home unattended."

"Come here." Events had transpired so quickly over the last few days that no real discussion had been had about Cordelia and Calem being . . . Whatever they were, but that didn't stop Calem from going over and giving her a huge hug. Cordelia was happy to accept, and she rested her head against his strong chest and closed her eyes for a second, allowing herself the comfort he was trying to give her. She didn't care that Haddie was there, she needed the security that Calem's embrace brought to her.

"Oh," Haddie said, not knowing how to react. Calem looked over at her and smiled, keeping Cordelia in his arms the entire time. When he let her go she felt more relaxed, but there was still a conversation that needed to be had.

"Are you okay to keep talking about it?"

"Yeah, we need to go over some things."

"I agree. The first thing I'm going to need is everything you have on 'Johnathan,' or whoever he said he was. That's the best place to start, even if he gave false information the guy exists. He was here, after all. Haddie hung out with him. We need to find him and bring him in."

"And you need a security system, ASAP," Haddie added.

"Don't worry about that, I'll get a detail on your place, but I don't think he'll be coming back here, he'd have to be crazy."

"He is," Cordelia said. "He'd have to be."

After all the information had settled in Cordelia just wanted to be alone. Haddie was going out again, so the place was free for a quiet evening with Calem. He made all the necessary calls and started a process that Cordelia knew wouldn't be quick, but it made her feel better knowing steps were being taken. She honestly didn't care about her own safety; that part of it never factored into her panic or anxiety, she was pissed, and she didn't want any other women to suffer what Sophia had gone through. She also felt guilty, even though she knew it was irrational.

After Haddie left for the evening Calem and Cordelia went upstairs to her bedroom to relax. It was well deserved after the day they had, and there wasn't anything more comforting than an evening in bed with a hot guy like him. She grabbed a bottle of Pinot from her wine collection in the kitchen and brought it upstairs with two glasses and a corkscrew, while Calem took off his work clothes, leaving him only in a pair of boxer briefs and a black tank top undershirt. He opened the bottle of wine for her, and poured them each a drink. "What a fucking day," he said while letting out a huge deep breath. "This one will go down in the history of bad days, huh?"

"No kidding," she said. "But I'm done feeling sorry for myself. It's not about my stress level. I know it's dumb, and I know you'll tell me I'm crazy, but I feel responsible for this somehow. Not just for Sophia, either, I feel responsible for all of it."

"You're right, that is dumb, and I'm not going to call you crazy, but you are taking this way too personally."

"How could I not?" she asked. "Let's say my hunch is correct, and it isn't just some wild coincidence that he knew about the Amazon package, and he is the guy."

"Okay."

"Well, if that's the case, then I've literally had the most wanted criminal in the city sitting across from me before most of the assaults happened, and I never suspected a thing. That's insane."

"It is," Calem agreed. "I'm not going to lie, it's like out of a movie or something, but that still doesn't put any responsibility on you. You know who else saw Johnathan? Everyone. A bunch of people saw him at Starbucks, or when he went to a movie, or when he ordered a pizza. The guy's not living in a cave in Afghanistan planning assaults; he lives in a city of millions of people. If he's the guy, he's interacted with way more people than you. You have to understand that."

"I get it," she said. "And I appreciate you trying to make me feel better, but the barista at Starbucks or the guy ripping his movie stub doesn't have a job where they're supposed to read people. That's what I do for a living; that's what I'm known for. - I'm good at my job and being able to tell how people really are as human beings, despite any facades or defense mechanisms they throw up. And I bought his act; I played into the fact that he was just an annoying guy who was failing as an author, when God knows who he really is or what he really does."

"That's fair enough, but even so, you have to follow the advice that you gave me, or it's worthless," said Calem.

"What do you mean?"

"How can you expect me to come out of my depression, and release my own guilt about not catching him sooner, if you're just going to turn around and put all that shit on yourself? You should really have a session with Dr. Summers. Have you met her, she's very insightful." Cordelia smiled. "I know her pretty well, and I'm no psychologist, but I'm pretty sure that if you told her how you were feeling, she might advise you that you're not magical, and that no one is responsible for a person's actions except that person, themselves."

"That sounds like good advice."

"Oh, it is. She said something similar to me once, and amazingly, it made me feel better. It made me remember that I can't control the evils of this world by myself, all I can do is whatever damage control is in my power to achieve, and that was a comforting thought. You should meet her."

She loved what he was doing; he wasn't the warm and fuzzy type, but he was just like her in wanting to make people feel better. It was working. "You're amazing," she said, leaning in for another hug.

"I know," he joked. "That goes without saying, but thanks."

"And by amazing I meant 'arrogant prick,' and you're welcome. I'll try, okay."

"Do you need me to quote Yoda right now?"

"How's that?"

"Do or do not, there is no try," he said in his best Yoda voice. He leaned down and kissed her softly and they both laid down on the bed. Sex could be many things, and none of them were mutually exclusive. It could be a purely physical act about the raw attraction between two bodies; it could be the physical expression of pure love or other emotions; and sometimes it could just be fun and comforting. Sex could also be an escape; an act that required the highest level of focus to do correctly, and whose physical reward could make those having it forget the evils of the world, at least for a little while. Being with Calem last night was the release of an emotional build up that announced the beginning of a new type of relationship with him. But tonight was different; tonight, she needed to escape, and get lost in the expanse of his body and the sensations he could bring to hers.

When they were both satiated Calem fell asleep. *Typical man*, she thought. Sex woke her up, how does it put him to sleep? But she envied his calm. It was exactly like he said; a few days ago she was comforting him; assuring him that he was doing his best, and that this guy's reign of terror would come to an end. Now the tables were turned, and it was she who needed reassurance, which he had done a great job in offering. While he lay there she took a moment to look over and just stare at his naked body. He was beautiful. Strong, chiseled, basically everything a man should be, and he was hers. The first time had been amazing, but now there was something deeper developing between them, and she felt as strong of an emotional connection as she did a physical one.

Getting up from bed she grabbed a tee shirt from her dresser and walked to her bedroom window. It was late, and the darkness was interrupted only by the streetlights and the moon above. Darkness. It hid so much, didn't it? But so did the light. The light hid people's awareness of the monsters of this world; one of whom was still out there, pleased with himself that he was still a free man. *We'll get you, you son of a bitch.*

CHAPTER EIGHTEEN

The cops picked up Johnathan the next day. The address Cordelia had on file was strangely his actual address. Calem got the call early, and had left before the sun had even risen. This time he woke Cordelia instead of leaving a note, he thought she'd want to know. "We got him," he said when she first opened her eyes. "I have to go in now, but I'll let you know as soon as we know anything else." It was nice to hear, but there were a lot of steps left between Johnathan sitting in an interrogation room and him locked behind bars forever, but this was a promising first step. Cordelia took solace in the small victory, but she was still utterly disturbed by everything.

She considered canceling her sessions, but she thought that helping others and getting her mind off of her own issues would be a sort of self-therapy she needed. It had been a few weeks since she had just purely enjoyed her job, and the act of helping people was something that brought her joy. Six one-hour sessions with a one hour break in between felt like a packed day—which it was—but it really kept her mind off things. In between each session, she checked her phone to see if there was any news, but so far there were no texts and no missed calls. Every hour on the hour she looked, trying not to obsess over what was happening at the police station but not being able to help it.

She knew Calem would reach out as soon as there was anything to discuss, but she was coming to the end of a seven-hour day and still nothing at all. She thought about texting him, but decided it was better to just let him do his job. He wanted this as much as she did, and she knew that; she had to trust him.

Just when she was losing hope that anyone would notify her, her phone buzzed. It was a text from Calem, but not the text that she was hoping for. All it read was: I'm almost at your place, I'll explain when I get there, I have a surprise for you. That was about as cryptic as a text could get, and it left so much open to interpretation that Cordelia decided that it was best to not even try to guess what he was alluding to. She hated surprises.

He was a man of his word, arriving less than ten minutes after she got his text. He looked exhausted, and there was nothing about his expression or body language that told her *We got him*! Instead of asking, Cordelia decided to just let him tell her whatever had transpired that day at the station. "Hey," he said. "How are you?"

"I'm doing okay, thanks for asking. I've been nervous on and off all day, but I saw a lot of patients to keep my mind focused elsewhere."

"That was smart. I wanted to text you earlier than I did, but to tell you the truth these things don't happen like you see on TV. Its not like you get the guy in a room, ask a couple of clever questions, and the guy just spills his guts."

"Yeah, I figured. So what actually happened then?"

"We had to let him go, Cordelia, I'm sorry." He hated saying those words to her, and he hated hearing them come from his mouth, but it was better to just be blunt and deal with the aftermath.

"What the fuck!"

"I know, I'm right there with you, trust me. But we had no choice but to cut him loose. We couldn't find anything on him."

Cordelia couldn't believe her ears. "After an entire day of having that man in custody the police couldn't find a single thing to hold him on? How is that possible?"

"It's not as simple as you'd think, Cordelia, there are aspects of this process you have to understand."

"Like what?" she asked, the anger rising in her voice.

"Like there's no actual evidence against him. We brought him in for questioning based on something he said to you that no one else heard, or that alluded to a crime. He denied saying it, of course, and claimed that you had a vendetta against him because he verbally accosted you and slammed your door. He admitted to being your former patient, and to talking to you in front of your place, but he claims it was just a weird coincidence that he happened to have met your friend the night before."

"A coincidence, you've got to be fucking joking."

"I know," Calem said. "We all knew it was bullshit, trust me, but we can't arrest someone based on a hunch, or on hearsay."

"Hearsay?"

"Yes, that's basically what it is. I have no doubt that he said that to you, or that he's our guy, but I can't arrest him if there's no other evidence against him except that."

"What about searching his house? Or his car? Something where you might find evidence of his crimes."

"Same thing as I was saying before about real life being different from television. Search warrants are issued by judges, and no judge in the world is going to sign a warrant for a search of a person's home or car without probable cause. And we don't have any physical evidence that would meet that legal standard."

"You sound like a lawyer right now."

"What I sound like is someone who understands this process. I'm just delivering the message, Cordelia, I didn't create this situation. You don't have to raise your voice to me like it's my fault." She was taken back when he said that. She knew that she was taking her emotions out on the wrong person when she saw the strained look on his face. She knew that she was being too harsh and a little bit selfish. She had made this whole thing about her, when in reality Calem had been invested in this case long before Cordelia even knew about it.

"I'm sorry, Calem." She could feel the frustrated tears welling up in her eyes, and before the first one could slide down her face Calem was holding her. He hated all of this. He hated that there were people like

Johnathan Kenenna who existed in the same world as people like Cordelia and Sophia; and he hated that he couldn't catch him for all the women who have been his victims. He held her tightly, reassuring her that it would be okay, that they would get him eventually, and that now the game had changed.

"Don't apologize, I get it. And look, we didn't get what we wanted today, but that piece of shit tipped his hand way too early. Now we know who he is, where he lives, all that. He knows that even though he could slip away from us on legal technicalities, he's got enough heat on him to start a forest fire." Cordelia started to giggle when he said that last part; she couldn't help it. "What?" he asked.

"Enough heat to start a forest fire?"

"Are you making fun of my comforting metaphor?"

"No . . ." She couldn't hold back the laughter anymore, and now that Calem heard it repeated back to him he realized how stupid it sounded, and he started cracking up too.

"Okay, okay, I'll work on my metaphors, I promise. But you know what I mean. He knows that we know, and that's to our advantage. At the very least we can keep enough eyes on him to prevent him from taking any risky moves. And starting tomorrow I'm going to have a patrol car do a drive by past your place a few times a day just to check up."

"I guess that's something," Cordelia said. "But Sophia and all the other women deserve better than that. They deserve justice."

"I know. They deserve to have him hanging by his balls. But if I've learned anything from this game, it's that you have to appreciate the small victories. Otherwise you'll go nuts."

"I guess. Hey, wait, you said that you had a surprise for me?"

"You're not going to like it."

"Then why call it a surprise? Surprises are supposed to be enjoyable, like something shiny from Tiffany."

"Something shiny from Tiffany," he repeated. "I'll remember that, but I have something much less . . . traditional."

"Okay, I'm intrigued, what've you got in that bag?" She noticed the bag when he first walked into her kitchen, but she didn't say anything. It looked large, and very un-present like.

"I'm taking you out on a date. A weird one."

"Okay," she said. "I'm a little interested and a little afraid at the same time. Are we going hiking up the vast hills of the upper west side?"

"Well, you're not that far off," he joked.

"Oh Jesus, I was kidding. Seriously, what the hell is in that bag?"

"Before I show you, you have to agree to keep an open mind."

"I agree to no such thing. I'll keep my mind as closed as I want it to be, depending on what's in there."

"The thing is . . ."

"Just show me, already, Calem, the buildup is killing me."

"All right then." Reaching behind himself, he picked up a giant gym bag. Cordelia could faintly see the color pink inside as Calem ruffled through the bag, and she could hear the meshing of plastic being gripped. Definitely not Tiffany, she thought, they don't sell big pink things in giant gym bags. When he pulled it out she just stared. He might as well have pulled a baby chimpanzee wrapped in a pink shirt out of that bag.

"What is it?" she asked.

"It's a Gi. A Jiu-Jitsu Gi, specifically."

"There are different types?"

"Yeah, but I won't bore you with the details."

"Is now the part where I ask why? Or are we still in the phase of our relationship where I smile and pretend to love everything you give me."

"Yes, we're still in that phase, for sure, so where's that fake smile?" Cordelia contorted her face into the creepiest high-cheeked smile her muscles would allow, and Calem started laughing uncontrollably. "Okay, I'm going to need you to stop making that face right now. I'll take the Gi back."

"Why," she joked, contorting her face even more. "I love it so much. I've always wanted a scrunched up pink robe for a martial art I know nothing about. And here I thought it was going to be jewelry. This is a great surprise after all."

"Shut up," he said, laughing.

"No, no, it's the best thing ever, seriously. Let me give you a kiss to thank you." She was still making the frozen, creepy face, and he shoved the Gi in her face to avoid the kiss.

"Can I explain?"

"I think that you have to, Calem. I'm curious."

"Do you know anything about jujitsu? You know, that 'chopsaki' stuff I do?"

"I think we've established my complete lack of martial arts knowledge, but go on, I live for lectures on fighting stuff."

"No lecture, just a lesson," he said.

"Wait, now!"

"Well, about a half hour or some from now, but this evening, for sure. I reserved the mats in the back just for us. I wanna show you a few things."

"This isn't like some kinky sex thing, is it? Not that I'm opposed to that; in fact, it would be preferable to actual Jiu-Jitsu. Is 'mats' code for suite at the Four Seasons, and Jiu-Jitsu code for . . . Well, whatever you want."

"Let's come back to this little fantasy later, but in this case, I'm speaking literally. You're going to take an actual, legit BJJ lesson, from me, and then your handsome and brave instructor is going to take you out to a nice dinner."

"I like that part," she said, trading her fake creepy smile for a real one. "Now, if only it didn't come after a thing I don't want to do."

"I think you'll like this. Remember that thing about keeping an open mind."

"I do," she answered. "Remember the part where I didn't promise to do it?"

"Touché," he joked. "Now let's go. But try this on first, I want to make sure I got the right size."

"I can't believe I'm doing this."

CHAPTER NINETEEN

G yms had a smell all their own, and martial arts gyms even more so. If you trained with any sort of regularity you didn't notice the offensive combo of sweaty men, rubber, and leather, but to the unindoctrinated newbies like Cordelia, the first fight at the gym would be against her own nostrils. "This whole place needs a shower," she said as they walked through the door. "How does it smell so bad and there's barely any one here but us."

"Maybe it's you," Calem joked. The place was practically empty; the last class ending over an hour ago. Calem had been training here for years. But tonight wasn't about belts, or classes, or even learning; tonight was about keeping Cordelia safe, whether she wanted to be taught or not. The Gi fit perfectly, and she had kept her pants on after changing at the apartment just in case she didn't feel like changing at the gym. The jacket was another thing, once she had it on it felt like she was transformed from a mild-mannered New York psychologist into a Texas armadillo. It was a shell; stiff in the collar, and hot as all hell in a place with no functioning air conditioning. "They can be a little stiff at first," he said.

"I see that," she said, giving him the look of death. "This restaurant you're going to take me to afterwards better be something mighty special." He smiled at her awkwardly, but she was still giving him the look. He was amazed at his powers of persuasion to even get her on a Jiu-Jitsu mat on a random night, with all that was going on. He was sure the offer of dinner sweetened the pot, but there was a method to his madness, always.

"So, you ready for your first lesson?"

"Let's do this already."

"When you see Jiu-Jitsu today you mostly see professional fighters using it. What the guys in the UFC and other martial arts organizations do when the fighter hits the ground to submit to their opponent, but it was actually developed for people to defend themselves against larger, stronger opponents."

"How does that work?" she asked.

"Well it doesn't use strikes, like punches and kicks. It's grappling, like wrestling or judo, so you have to grab onto your opponent and try to make them give up by chocking them or threatening to break one of their limbs."

"Sounds violent," she said.

"Actually, it's called the *gentle art*."

"Make sense," she said, the sarcasm meter starting to grow. "I like to break limbs gently. You know, so the guy attacking me doesn't think I'm too manly."

"I love that good attitude you promised."

"I didn't promise."

"Whatever, get over here."

She was giving him all kinds of shit because it was amusing, but she got right away what he was doing and why he was doing it. Even with a police detail and heat from the cops, Johnathan Kenenna was still out there, and for some reason he had an interest in Cordelia. She had been to some bullshit self-defense courses before; her dad practically forced her to take one when she told him that she was moving into the city alone. The class had been total garbage. Some steroid freak teaching a bunch of women to kick a guy in the balls, scream "no," and carry pepper spray in their bags for protection. Even as a young novice with no fight experience, Cordelia knew that if shit ever really went down she could never use anything that guy had taught her. BJJ, on the other hand . . . "You do this with Jesse?" she asked.

"Yeah, he's getting really good for a newer guy, actually. Why?"

"This seems a little . . . I don't know, intimate."

Calem smiled. That wasn't the word he would have chosen but he understood why she said that. Grappling in general, and BJJ in particular, was a close up, body-to-body activity, and as Cordelia found her head between Calem's legs for a triangle choke, she couldn't help but picture him and his partner. "Do you ever think this may be why you and I took so long to get together?"

"Why's that?" he asked, opening his legs so she could breathe.

"Well, I don't know, maybe you've been exploring alternative lifestyles with your partner? And hey, no judgment here, it's just an interpretation."

"I see, and is that your professional evaluation, Dr. Summers?"

"Just a working theory, not conclusive. There's evidence to the contrary."

They both giggled. Calem wanted to keep it playful yet serious. He didn't want to make this into another self-defense experience like she had, but he did want her to actually learn a few techniques in case she needed them. And she was actually a good student. He showed her the basics and, like all good students, she asked a bunch of questions. *So where does my right arm go to secure the choke? What happens if I move this way instead of that way? Why do you need to grip your hands together for that move?* Calem was impressed. Not only did she grasp some of the basic principles of Jiu-Jitsu faster than some blue belts he knew, she wanted to drill them over and over again.

An hour and a half after they had walked in Cordelia was exhausted but stopped only grudgingly. She had learned a lot, and was amazed that she had gone in with such a bad attitude. Calem went through the basic stuff about keeping close to someone attacking you so they couldn't hit you, as well as two basic submissions that they drilled over and over again. Cordelia was sweating through her new pink Gi, breathing more heavily than she had since her ill-planned phase of running the New York City Marathon last year (which she never did). The lesson was that she needed to get in better shape, but she kinda liked this Jiu-Jitsu thing. And, more importantly, she loved that Calem was teaching her something out of pure concern for her safety.

The place was dark except for a few overhead lights that the gym owner had left on after the last class had ended. Calem had the keys and instructions to lock up when he and his "lady friend," as the gym owner had referred to Cordelia, were done. Besides enough light to keep the mats and each other visible, the building was completely dark. From the backroom they were practicing in you could see the street through the glass widow, and the moving lights of the city were vaguely perceptible. "You did great," Calem said. "You're a natural."

"I had a good teacher, but thank you. I liked it."

"Maybe I can get you down here regularly. You know, even when we're not all in danger."

"We'll see about that. Let's just start with me liking my first lesson and go from there."

"Fair enough," he said, happy that she was into it. "Wanna go to dinner?"

"Not just yet," she said. Cordelia reached across and grabbed the lapel of Calem's Gi, her arm deep inside of the collar, and she pulled him down on top of her. She remembered the "guard" position, and wrapped her legs around his waist, locking her ankles together and squeezing her legs. She had a tight grip for someone who'd never done this before, and she pulled his head down sharply until it was just an inch above hers. Her hand came out from his collar and wrapped around the back of his neck; her legs tightening their squeeze around his torso. The last inch of the descent was all Calem's, and he turned his head as he moved down so their lips could meet and press together. He kept kissing her even harder, until she pulled away after a few seconds. "We're not having sex on some nasty mat, covered in sweat, just so you know."

"Thank you for that information," he joked, "And nice tight guard, by the way."

"Thank you." She said, smiling.

"And speaking of information, did you know that Jesse's taking Haddie out?"

"What? Why do you know this and I don't?"

"Couldn't tell you," he said. "But he tells me they're going out tomorrow. I guess he stopped saying stupid shit to her finally."

"Wow, good for him. And her. I'm a little pissed that she didn't tell me though."

"Does she tell you a lot?" he asked.

"Not so much, now that you mention it. Even back in college she was always a little . . ."

"Secretive?"

"Not secretive. More guarded. Private. Wouldn't offer much about her life unless you asked her a few times directly. She's always been more of the free spirit, fun loving type, but she keeps her distance sometimes. That's why I try not to take things like this personally. She's like that with everyone."

"You're right, don't take it personally, some people are just like that. Plus, if anyone will ask her direct questions it's Jesse. He's too much of a cop and too crazy to realize that she's a private person. He'll ask her life story within the first fifteen minutes of whatever it is they're doing."

"Good luck to him, then. Maybe he'll learn a few things I don't know."

"Maybe," Calem said smiling. "Or maybe he'll just act like an idiot. You can never quite tell."

"He's not an idiot; we had a talk the other day."

"When did you two talk?" Calem asked.

"Outside of the station. We had a mini therapy session."

"With Jesse?" he asked, sounding very surprised.

"You're the best listener ever," she joked. "Yes, with Jesse. He was very expressive with me, there were a few things he needed to get off of his chest—none of which I can tell you about, of course. But he was hardly an idiot; he surprised me."

"If it's what I think it was that he wanted to get off his chest, I'm glad he finally told someone else besides me. I'm glad that you were able to be there for him. You're amazing at what you do." Cordelia leaned over and kissed him again; a different kind of kiss this time; one that signified the deepest feelings.

"You already have me, you don't have to keep flattering me, you know."

"It's not about flattery," he said, looking deeply into her eyes. "I don't even think I know how to do that. It's the truth. You're a talented psychologist, and you help everyone who's smart enough to accept your help. I know that we never finished our sessions, but you helped me tremendously."

"Thank you." His words were music, and they served as validation for everything she tried to do as a psychologist. She had doubted herself as of late; not just because of Johnathan Kenenna, but in general. She felt stuck in the professional mud—like nothing she did made much difference in people's lives. But sitting there with him, in the most unusual of situations, and listening to his words help bring everything sharply into focus.

"You're welcome," he continued, "and I'm not just saying any of this to make you feel better. That's also something I don't do. For good or for bad I tell the truth, no matter what, and if I say that I'm a better man for having known you, then that's the truth. I'm a much better man now than I was before I knew you. You've given me a clarity that I haven't known for a very long time."

In her head, Cordelia knew what her next words were; she knew exactly how they sounded and how she should say them. The truth was that those words were always there, on the tip of her tongue recently, but they were powerful words that demanded the perfect placement, because without that, they could cause more harm than good. But something held her back; something kept her from articulating that which was in her heart and waiting in her mouth to come out. Then, surprisingly, it came from him.

"I love you, Cordelia. And I never thought I'd say that on the mat in the middle of an empty gym, but there are a lot of things between you and me that I never thought would happen, so why not say it now? I love you."

"I love you too, Calem." The words flowed out of her like they were meant to be said, and maybe they were. He'd always been her hero, starting from the first time they met and up to right now. The universe could be a funny place, she thought, from rescuing me from that guy, to coming up to me at a conference, and now here; Calem had been a fixture in her life for some time, and now she could express how she truly felt without holding anything back.

"Who would've thought we'd be here?"

"Not me," she said, but then realized she was lying a little bit. "Well, sort of."

"Sort of?" he asked.

"I always wanted you, Calem, whether you realized or not, but I'm not some desperate stalker. I didn't obsess, and I didn't pursue anything. I'm a scientist at heart, and I know what I'm about to say is about as un-scientific as it gets, but I really hoped that if I was patient that fate would just bring us together one day."

"And here we are. I wish I could believe in fate, but whatever it was that led us here, fate, coincidence, random acts of the universe, it doesn't matter, does it? Here we are."

"Here we are." They kissed one more time and then got changed. They both needed a shower in the worst way, but Calem needed to go back to his place to get some clothes. Outside the night air was cold for summer, and there was a dampness in the breeze that signaled rain. "It feels like October out here."

"Yeah, it's supposed to pour," Calem said. "Better get home before it does."

"I have an idea," she said. "Why don't you get changed and then come to my place. Bring some stuff."

"You mean, like, to stay over?"

"Uh-huh."

Calem felt really excited. He wasn't your typical man in any way, and not only wasn't he afraid of a committed relationship, he embraced every aspect of it. He didn't have too many close guy friends because he wasn't a fan of hitting up bars and trying to hook up with random girls. He got the appeal, sure, but it wasn't for him long-term. He loved being in love; loved having a girlfriend in every way, and it made him a much better version of himself than he was when he was single. He was telling the truth when he said he couldn't believe in fate—it never made much sense to him. But it was also true that he didn't care why they were together, only that they were. And as he kissed her one more time before heading home, he made a self-declaration in his mind, a mantra of sorts that was based on his newly developed self-awareness. *I will not mess this one up. I will not make my job more important than the future we could have.*

"I'll see you in a little. Give me like an hour or so."

"Take your time, I need a shower also."

And with one last kiss they went their separate ways, temporarily. Cordelia crossed her arms as she felt goose bumps popping up on each arm. The storm was on its way, and she hoped she could get home before it rained all over her.

CHAPTER TWENTY

As it turned out, Haddie wasn't hogging the bathroom at all, she was showered, dressed, and having a pre-date glass of wine in Cordelia's kitchen when she finally got home. She had beaten the rain by a few seconds, and even though it was nowhere near storm-levels of downpour, rhythmic drops were bouncing off of her windows. "You just made it, huh?" Haddie said.

"Yeah, I hear it's going to get bad out there."

"Shit, I have the worst luck."

"Why?" Cordelia asked, pretending to be ignorant of the situation. "Where are you off to?"

"Going out with Jesse. Calem's Jesse, can you believe that?"

"I could if you would've told me. Why no mention?" She tried to sound like she was joking, and she told Calem she wasn't going to take this personally, but she was a little hurt that her good friend kept so much to herself.

"Oh, I'm sorry, I didn't even think of it. You know how I am, I wasn't trying to keep it from you. I was exploring the city a little and there's this little boutique not far from the station, apparently. I was walking around the area after I got these shoes, and I bumped into him."

"How was that?" Cordelia asked, already knowing the answer.

"It was cool. He's cool. Not at all what he seemed like the other night. I mean, he was nice and all that, and he's a hot guy, but he was so awkward then. The other day he sounded like a normal guy. And he was bold enough to ask me out and I thought, why not?"

"I wonder what changed that made him less awkward?" Cordelia knew, of course, and even though dating hadn't been a focus of her little impromptu session at the deli with Jesse, she hoped it had helped with that also. It seemed to have. "Not that it matters, he's a great guy."

"Yeah, we'll see what happens."

"When are you leaving?" Cordelia asked.

"He should be here before too long, he sent me a text a few minutes ago saying he was getting ready to leave his place soon."

"Calem's coming over too. He's just getting changed."

"Speaking of keeping secrets," Haddie threw in. It was a pretty fair touché moment.

"What's the deal with that situation?"

"Not keeping secrets, it's just that everything happened kind of fast . . . Well, actually it happened kind of slow, but once he made the first move it went really fast."

"That's what it was like with my ex back in California. That can happen when you're friends with a guy first. Things escalate quickly because you already know a lot about each other, which is kind of the point of dating someone you don't already know. But once you start up with a friend it's just about compatibility and learning about each other in a totally different way, so that first part goes faster than normal." That made a lot of sense, and Haddie definitely had more experience dating than Cordelia did. They were the classic introvert/extrovert pair—balancing each other out pretty well while still being profoundly different people. It's what Cordelia loved about their friendship.

They shared a glass of wine since Haddie had already cracked open a bottle, and they spent a few minutes catching up on what each of them had been up to. It felt very normal and very familiar. So far, since Haddie had arrived the majority of their time had been spent apart. It felt good to catch up with one another, even if just for a few minutes over a glass of wine. "I need to take a shower before Calem gets here."

"I'm all set. Listen if I'm gone when you get out have a good night. Jesse should be here soon. I'll tell you all about it tomorrow."

"You'd better."

Cordelia left her friend in the kitchen with an empty wine glass that she planned on refilling while she waited for her date to arrive. When the doorbell rang a few minutes later Cordelia was already in the shower and Haddie was a little buzzed. Jesse was a little earlier than anticipated, but she was getting bored sitting around the house anyhow. "Hold on, I'm coming," she yelled. She was excited to see him, so she ran to the front door and opened it right up. By the time she realized that it wasn't Jesse, but Johnathan Kenenna standing in the doorway, it was too late. He pushed inside and threw her to the ground, shutting the front door behind him and locking it from the inside. She had time for one scream, just one. After that everything went black as Johnathan brought his fist down on her face as hard as he could, and she was knocked out cold.

He didn't waste any time going to work. With the twine he'd brought, he bound Haddie's hands behind her back, and dragged her by the hair into Cordelia's office. He had been waiting outside her place for a while, hiding in plain sight since the cops had sprung him loose earlier that day. He knew that this was the best time to strike because the police wouldn't expect anything from him right after hauling him down to the station.

He knew it was over, and that it had to end with a bang. He planned on a dramatic ending to all of his "work." No more random women at random apartments; he believed that it had to end with something so dramatic that they'd study his crimes for years. If he wanted to keep on he wouldn't have tipped his hand to Cordelia outside of her place. He knew that before he died tonight, he was going to take Cordelia and Haddie with him in one last dramatic act, and that there was nothing that piece of shit cop and his partner could do to stop him.

The gun in his pocket was loaded, ready to take out his last few victims, and then himself. He didn't know it would happen quite this fast, but this was his plan all along, to be remembered forever. Now he could complete the last part of his plan with little interruption. Or so he believed.

Cordelia took a quick shower by her standards, and twenty minutes later she was drying off and checking her phone to see if Calem had texted that he was on his way. Nothing so far. She figured she was alone at this point, with Haddie out painting the town red with poor Jesse, who had no idea what he was in for with her. But before she came out of her room naked she wanted to make sure there was no one else in the house. "Haddie?" she yelled with her bedroom door mildly cracked open. No response. I guess I have the place to myself for a few minutes, she thought, not knowing the nightmare that lurked only a few feet away.

Haddie had been incidental to Johnathan. She was only an entry point, an appetizer to the main course, which was Cordelia. He had no reason to hate her so vehemently; no reason to hate any of the women he had terrorized and traumatized, but looking for rational reasons in crimes like his was a fool's errand, and he was all the more frightening because it didn't make any sense at all outside of his twisted fucking head. Cordelia needed to double check. She was modest and thought she had heard some noise beneath her when she got out of the shower initially. So she threw on a long tee shirt and leaned out her bedroom door one more time, opening the door wider than she had before. "Hadd—"

Johnathan pushed her door in with all of his might, hitting her in the face and knocking her to the floor. The pain she felt was secondary to the shock she was experiencing; her nightmare staring down at her from above with a satisfied grin on his face. Cordelia wasn't a fighter by nature, but she was tough as nails, and the look on this guy's face made her as angry as it did afraid. "Where's Haddie?" she asked frantically, having little concern for herself at that moment and just wanting her friend to be okay.

"Out of the way, for now. But there's plenty of time to have fun with her later. But don't you worry, I came here for you, Dr. Summers, and you'll get all of my attention." His words chilled her to the core, not only because she knew how dangerous he was, but because she could read the insanity in his face. He didn't care anymore—he didn't care about covering his tracks, or getting arrested, or anything else that a normal person would be concerned about. He had no fear, and that made him ten times as dangerous as he already was. It was animal-like, but Cordelia understood that she was in a fight for her life, and she had to play her hand perfectly to make it out of there alive.

She could see the bulge of a gun under his shirt, and she assumed that he might have other weapons on him based on his crimes. He was also known for using whatever objects happened to be in the home he broke into to torture his victims. Nothing was out of the question. Lamps, broomsticks, kitchen utensils—in Johnathan Kenenna's hands anything could be a torture device. Cordelia's head was still buzzing from the blow she had taken, but she knew that she wasn't going out like a victim. As he ranted about how much she deserved what was about to happen, she settled her mind down and started doing what she did best, analyze the situation and read people. She noticed his clothes, the speed at which he was talking, the look in his eyes, everything. She also started to problem solve. *How can I get out of this? How strong is he? Should I run? What about Haddie?* It was in that brainstorm that she remembered the most obvious of things: there were two cops on their way over soon.

She knew Calem would arrive, for sure, but she knew less about Jesse's situation. Despite that, she understood that time was actually on her side here. If she could prevent the inevitable, or just survive for long enough, help was already on the way. She didn't need to call anyone, all she had to do was ride out the clock. "Johnathan, listen, I don't know what I ever did except try to help you."

"Help me?" he yelled. "Help me, you said? That's amazing, you delusional bitch. All you did was criticize, and tell me how whiny I was, and how I wasn't helping myself at all. And you call that help."

"That's not quite what I did, but okay."

"Shut up!" He wasn't in the mood for a robust debate about the nature of effective therapy; he was a man who hated women at his core, plain and simple, and who loved hurting them more than anything. The real reasons for that would never be known for sure; the actual therapy Cordelia could have done with him to figure that out was just a fantasy now, and she knew the pot for this game of poker was her life and the life of her best friend. She had to be careful.

"All right, I'm sorry. I'm sorry." She looked down to show submissiveness because she thought it might calm him slightly. She put up both hands in a show of surrender and tried to talk to him some more to waste time. All of this was a gamble, logic that may or may not work because it relied on rationality, something Johnathan was lacking at the moment.

"That's better," he said. "But it ain't gonna save you from what's coming. You can pretend to fight back if you want to, or you can play the damsel, but it's not gonna make a goddamn bit of difference in a few minutes when you're begging me to kill you." She didn't know how to react anymore. Her base impulse was to stand up and run. One last fight-or-flight burst of adrenaline that might save her from the horrors he was describing. But she remembered that she wasn't a cornered animal, she was an intelligent human being who could think and act, and that mattered here. As she was planning on what to do or say next, the front door rang. Oh shit, she thought, that's either Calem or Jesse, but which one is it . . .

Johnathan's boot hit her ribs so hard that she felt like his foot was inside of her. She'd always heard phrases like "I got the wind knocked out of me," but until she felt it she had no idea what it meant. She literally couldn't take in or let out air, not even to scream for help, so she curled into a defensive ball on the floor. "Stay here," he said, leaving the room as quickly as his feet could carry him.

Outside Jesse was feeling bad. He had finally managed to speak to the first girl he'd been legitimately interested in for a while, and now he was late picking her up. He didn't have any idea what was happening on the other side of that door, of course, nor what would happen when it finally opened. From where he stood he was just a guy who was late picking up what was most likely an annoyed girl, but he vowed to take her someplace nice to make up for it. When too much time passed without a response he rang a second time. "Haddie?" he yelled. "Jesus, am I that late?"

There was a window to the right of Cordelia's front door where you could see into her office. Normally she kept the shades down for privacy, but since she had cut back her schedule this week, she left it open. He didn't' know why he looked at that window and not the one that led into the kitchen; maybe it was just the cop in him, but he had been through enough situations to know when something might be wrong. He didn't know why, but a voice in his head told him to check that window. It wasn't easy. The blinds were partially closed and he had to lean his body to the point of almost falling over the steps to see, but when he did he reached for his gun. It was Haddie, and she was tied up and limp on the floor.

He slammed his shoulder into the door without thinking, and the door flew open with some force. Jesse didn't hear the shot that hit him square in the stomach, but he felt it. He had been shot before—in Afghanistan—but it was in the leg and only a flesh wound. That was years ago. He had never taken a shot directly in the line of duty. It felt warm and tingly; the pain coming later, and before falling to the floor he reached for his gun and got a shot off in Johnathan's direction. He missed and hit the wall, but he wasn't going down without a fight.

He was shot, but he wasn't down yet. Jesse McMann was many things, but easy to take out was not one of them. He had been to some of the darkest places in the world and faced some of the worst human beings while in the service, and some asshole with a 38caliber was not going to end it all without a fight. Moving on pure adrenaline and instinct, Jesse pulled his own gun and pointed it towards Johnathan, firing indiscriminately in his general direction two times. He wasn't going for accuracy as much as he was for distraction. If he hit the guy, great, but he was returning fire so that he could move forward without taking another slug to the stomach or chest.

Upstairs Cordelia could hear the shots, and she started panicking at what might be happening in her living room. Downstairs, Jesse was fighting for his life. Charging the Manhattan rapist while shot in the stomach, he lunged forward and caught the man in a clinch. Each man still had his gun in hand, and each was struggling to gain an advantage. In a normal situation Jesse would have easily had the physical advantage. He was much larger than Johnathan - outweighing him by about twenty pounds, and he was skilled in grappling and other hand to hand combat. But a bullet in the stomach was a game changer, no matter how much adrenaline your body was pumping to suppress the pain.

Johnathan realized this, and took full advantage of the situation. As their hands were tied up in a stalemate of grabbing at each other's weapons, Johnathan brought his right knee up into Jesse's stomach with full strength, and the wounded detective buckled to the floor, screaming in excruciating pain. It seemed like it was all over, but as Johnathan started to turn his gun on the detective he heard a loud bang from upstairs. *Cordelia*, he thought, *I've got to go finish that bitch off!* He didn't have time for Jesse now – he was just extra. No, Johnathan came for her, and he knew as far as Jesse went the bullet would do its job. *Let the pig bleed*, he thought before kicking Jesse in the face. Johnathan pushed the door closed with his foot. It was over now. Shots had been fired, there were witnesses passing by on the street, and he had shot a cop. Johnathan knew this was the end, and that made him all the more dangerous.

As Jesse lay on the floor bleeding and Haddie was unconscious in the office, Cordelia got up and texted Calem. Johnathan was getting sloppy, and he didn't bother to check her for a phone, or bind her limbs in any way. She was still feeling the effects of what were most likely some broken ribs, but she was mobile. She thought about escaping through her bedroom window and yelling for help, but she couldn't leave Haddie. She heard the shot that had just rung out through the entire house and didn't know if her friend was still alive, or if that maniac had killed Jesse.

A minute after the two shots downstairs had rung out she heard his footsteps approaching. Those boots that had shattered her ribs were loud, and she hid behind the door as the steps got more and more audible. She heard him right on the other side of the door and she held her breath in anticipation as he stepped through. She didn't think, she just ran and jumped on his back. His gun fell and hit the ground and she held onto him for dear life, clawing at his face. He turned into her and they both fell to the ground. She hit the back of her head when they fell, and she immediately felt dizzy, but without even thinking she kept a grip on his jacket and wrapped her legs around him tightly. He tried to lean up and punch her but she kept control of his head, squeezing it to her chest like her life depended on it. She knew that if he could sit up he could easily punch her in the face, or worse, so she just tried to keep him as tied up as her weakened body would allow. It wasn't easy.

He was strong; made even stronger by the desire he had to hurt her, and as he pulled to slip his head out of her grip, she poured every last bit of strength her body had into keeping him down. She knew she couldn't keep it up for long, and knew that when she relaxed her body it was all over, so she just kept squeezing until her body forced her to relent. The entire time Johnathan was struggling he was threatening her life, calling her horrific names, and describing how he was going to kill her once he got free of her grasp. She felt her arms failing her; he was just too strong and too angry, and she was diminished from the broken ribs and the dizziness. Reluctantly, she felt her legs break open, and when they did he just stood up over her, breaking the grip she had on his head easily. She didn't have anything left, not even enough energy to stand up and run away, so she laid there, preparing for the worst.

Johnathan pulled out what looked to be about a three-inch knife from the inside of his jacket and held it over her. "It's time now," he said with a crazy look in his eyes. As he was about to bring the blade down into Cordelia's chest, the bullet from Calem's chamber found its way across the room, burying itself inside Johnathan's black heart. His body flew backward from the impact, and he fell to the floor, dead from a single shot. Calem ran to the floor and grabbed a hold of Cordelia, pulling her upright. "Are you hurt?" he asked frantically.

"My ribs, and I hit my head on the floor, but I'm alive. The others?"

"Haddie's hurt but okay, and I called a bus for Jesse. I have to go tend to his wounds right now, but I'll carry you down."

"I love you, Calem."

"I love you too. Don't talk, okay, save your strength. It'll all be okay."

"You were right, you know?"

"About what?"

"That chopsaki stuff. It kind of works."

It was nearly impossible to smile in a situation like they had been in, but she found a way to make him do just that. Everyone was going to be fine, but there was a long road to recovery ahead.

The New York News

Last night yet another reign of terror came to an end thanks to Detective Calem Walters, and his partner, Detective Jesse McMann. In a bizarre set of circumstances Detective McMann was critically wounded after encountering the suspected Manhattan Rapist, whose name is Johnathan Kenenna. In a scuffle at the home of a local psychologist, Dr. Cordelia Summers, the detectives attempted to rescue their colleague and her roommate from an attack by Kenenna, who was killed by a single gunshot wound to the heart.

The NYPD Police Commissioner made the following statement at a press conference this morning:

"For their bravery, both Detective Walters and Detective McMann will be awarded the police combat cross for their extreme acts of heroism under the imminent threat of death, and for their rescue of two civilians in the process. These two detectives represent everything the NYPD expects of New York's finest, and I am personally honored to know both men. The city owes them a tremendous debt that can never be repaid, and we all wish Detective McMann a speedy recovery from the injuries he sustained."

CHAPTER TWENTY-ONE

A Month Later

"They keep calling me a hero. You know how I hate that."

"I do know, but they don't. They're being nice to you and, by the way, you fit the definition perfectly, so just smile and say, 'thank you.' Incidentally, why do you dislike praise so much?"

"That question made you sound so much like a shrink it's ridiculous," Calem commented. He was right, and in the dichotomy that was Cordelia and Dr. Summers she was about at an eighty twenty split in favor of the latter. She was back to giving therapy sessions today after recovering from her injuries, and seeing a therapist herself for some of the trauma she experienced. She felt bad redirecting all of her patients to colleagues for a few weeks, but she knew that if she didn't get her head right she'd be no good helping anyone else. But a month was enough to start on the road to recovery, and her first patient was her boyfriend, Detective Calem Walters, the man who saved her life.

Boyfriend. That was still a little weird to hear in her own head. *I'm seeing my boyfriend Calem for a therapy session.* She was getting used to it, though. Their relationship had developed from a strong friendship and collegial pairing into the most ideal romance either of them had ever known. It was a strange journey down a winding road, but both of them were filled with excitement about what the future brought. "I am a shrink. And there's a word I hate, which is much worse than 'hero,' but stop evading. Why don't you accept praise easily?"

"If it softens the blow you're the hottest shrink in the tristate area, at least. Maybe the country. And to answer your question, it's like I've told you before, it's not that I have trouble accepting praise, per se, it's more like I have trouble being lionized."

"Big word for a cop."

"Too much sarcasm for a shrink." He smiled when he said that one so she'd know he was joking, and she did the same. "But, seriously, if a person whose life I impacted in some way wants to thank me I'm more than happy to accept that, even though it's not necessary. But it's the label I reject—calling me a hero for doing my job just seems silly to me. It's not a label any real hero wants."

"So, you think of yourself as a hero, you just don't like to be called on it?"

"Yes. No. Sort of. I mean . . . Can I just kiss you now, my head hurts from all the therapy."

"Um, we're in session, detective. I don't know how you treat your other doctors, but I hope you don't ask to kiss them when you don't like how your session is going."

"My medical doctor is an eighty-one year-old-man who I've seen forever. I mean, I've tried to kiss him a few times as a thank you, but it just got plain uncomfortable."

"Stop," she said, laughing hysterically.

"People can call me whatever they want, but I'll never get used to praise for just doing what I signed up to do for a living. I never want to get used to that."

"I understand," she said. "That makes sense. How's Jesse?"

"Sore, but doing well. The bullet missed all of his vital organs, so it was just a really painful shot. He's going to be at one hundred percent when he's all healed up, but he's still recovering at home. He's got an in-home nurse catering to his every need."

"Plus Haddie"

"Plus Haddie, yeah. Funny how things work out," he said.

"He did save her life; you both saved our lives in different ways at different times. If Jesse hadn't rung the bell when he did, Johnathan might have tried to kill me then and there in my room. Him leaving to shoot Jesse gave me time to text you and get myself ready to fight."

"And fight you did. You should get your blue belt automatically just for grappling the Manhattan Rapist."

"I didn't do it that well," she added. "If it hadn't been for good timing and a good shot on your part I'd have been on the business end of that blade he brought."

"Let's not think about all that anymore. It's over."

"It is over, but then why did you want to see me. I hope you're over Tori at this point or we're gonna need to have some follow up sessions."

"Who?"

"Good boy."

"No, it's not about her or what happened with Johnathan. It's something else I've been thinking a lot about, and I wanted to pick your brain."

"Pick away," she said.

"I'm thinking about retirement." It was a shock to hear him say those words, and she leaned forward in her chair without even realizing it.

"What? Why?"

"You forgot who, when, and where."

"Stop joking, what are you talking about?"

"I joined the force when I was twenty-one, just out of high school, literally. I'm close to the end of my career anyhow. I know I could go longer, but I think next year is it for me. I'm going to put in my papers."

"I guess if that's what is in your heart then it's the right thing. It's not the kind of job where you can be half in and half out."

"Exactly, and you kind of inspired me a little bit." Cordelia raised her eyebrow at him. "Okay, a lot, actually."

"How did I do that?"

"There's always going to be another monster out there. When you shove almost two million people into an area that's twenty-four miles across, you're going to have a lot of crime."

"And over three million with commuters during the day."

"Right. The NYPD will be fine, there are some great young guys out there to keep the universe in balance. I can't fight that fight forever without it taking something from me. There'll always be another monster, but I don't think I want to keep fighting them forever."

After listening closely to everything he was saying, Cordelia got up and gave Calem a huge hug. "I think that makes perfect sense. You know you have my support, always, but I wanted to hear the why. I wanted to make sure you weren't running away because of what almost happened to me or Haddie."

"I don't run, Cordelia, and you should always know that about me. In fact, the only way I run is toward the danger and toward the challenge. But I want to have a part of my life that's not dedicated to chasing the scum of the earth. I want a normal life with you."

A normal life with you. If she was being honest with herself she wanted to hear those words, and she wanted the same. Their relationship was still in its infancy, but she knew that time was no indicator of a successful relationship. There were people married for twenty years getting divorced, and kids who married at nineteen who stayed married forever. It wasn't about time, it was about the person looking across from you, and how badly you wanted them in your life. There were no words that could communicate her response to that, but a kiss could do all the talking. "So, I have to put up with you never being around for another year?"

"I'll be around. I'll do my job like I've always done it, but I'll do a better job at balancing it all, now that I have something worth balancing it with."

They kissed one more time, to seal the deal. "Our time is just about up, detective."

"Any plans for the rest of the day? Seeing more patients?"

"No, you're my only today; I wanted to start back slow and build. Tomorrow's a full calendar. I'm happy, though, I missed doing what I love to do. I just needed some time to recover but I know we'll all be happy to reunite and do some hard work together."

"I like the sound of that," he said. "And speaking of hard work, you owe me some sessions—on the mat!"

"Is that, like a sexual innuendo?"

"Of course, but also I mean it literally. You have a natural talent for grappling, you need to come down with me and take home some limbs of unsuspecting guys."

"I might just have to do that. But not today. I'm going to get lunch and hang out with Haddie. She's been with Jesse a lot but he's at physical therapy this afternoon, so she's free."

"How's she doing?"

"Better," Cordelia answered. "Much better, actually. For her it was just the emotional scarring of it all. Plus the guilt she felt."

"What did she have to feel guilty about?"

"Noting, really, but she felt like she was stupid for hanging out with Johnathan and bringing him to my doorstep—literally. I told her none of this is her fault. But we're gonna move on to happier things."

"Say hi for me, and we'll all hang out soon—the four of us—once my partner is back to his old self again."

"Sounds like a plan."

They kissed one more time before Calem left for training, and Cordelia followed him out to grab an Uber to meet Haddie. She was still living with Cordelia, but was actively looking for a place. Cordelia was happy to have her, and she honestly liked having the company. After the shooting, Cordelia had to be out of her place for a few weeks while the cops did their thing at the crime scene, so she had stayed with Calem while Haddie stayed at Jesse's while he recovered. But now things were slowly getting back to normal, and there was nothing more normal than a glass of wine and a great lunch with a friend.

It took fifteen minutes for her Uber to navigate the early afternoon Manhattan traffic, but she got there right on time, and Haddie was already seated outside. "Pinot?" Cordelia asked, seeing the already poured glass of red sitting across from Haddie.

"Of course, did you even need to ask?"

"I guess not," she said. "How's our boy?"

"Good. He said hi and that he wants to get together with the four of us when he's better."

"I think Calem and him share a brain sometimes, Calem just said the same to me at the end of our session."

"Your session? You're still counseling your boyfriend? That's got to be a little awkward."

"Actually," Cordelia started, reflecting back on the few times they'd spoken, "it's not awkward at all. We've had some great conversations, and he's been completely open with me."

"That's rare for a cop, you're lucky he's like that with you."

The waitress came over mid-conversation and took their order. Haddie was eating light. "Watching your girlish figure?" she asked.

"No, just not that hungry."

"Everything okay?" Cordelia asked.

"Yeah, I'm good, just worried about Jesse. He's been a little messed up since everything happened."

"Well of course he has, I think we all have in one way or another."

"Not physically. And not even psychologically for the reasons you might think."

"Try me."

"He feels like he let everyone down; that he missed his chance to save the day and just got shot instead. He feels like it was his job to save us, and it was just dumb luck that Calem showed up when he did. He feels like he almost got us both killed."

"God, these two really take the weight of the world on their shoulders, don't they? So much guilt for no reason."

"They're cops, it's what they do. It's why they became what they became."

"You speak the truth," Cordelia said. "But it's our jobs to keep them grounded and to remind them that they're just men. They shouldn't be so hard on themselves."

"Good luck winning that argument," Haddie said, flagging down the waitress for a refill.

"I win them over with reason and understanding. It's the only way to get through to them. If you just try to tell someone that they're wrong about how they feel, then they shut off right away. If you try to empathize and understand where they're coming from first, then they'll usually listen to what you have to say. That goes for anyone, not just cops. If he ever needs to speak to anyone my door's always open."

"I should give that a try. I'm more the first one—the judgmental one—but I guess that explains a lot of my past relationships. And it explains why you're so popular."

"Please don't use that word, it makes me sound like the prom queen of psychologists."

"I'm cracking up thinking about you as the prom queen."

"Me too. So where are things with you and Jesse? I know he's recovering but are you guys a thing?"

"I honestly don't know what we are. We never really got started. I like him, but I've been hanging out with him because I feel bad. He got shot because of me . . . sort of. I'd feel like an asshole if I just walked away from him. But we never really got to explore what we could be."

"There's time," Cordelia assured her. "There's always time."

They finished their lunches and went their separate ways, with a promise to find a movie for a girl's night in later; their own little *Netflix and Chill* session. It was too nice of a day for another Uber, so instead Cordelia decided to take a few minutes and appreciate the city that she lived in. A lot of the stereotypes about Manhattan were true: life was fast paced, people were always moving, and everyone was focused on their own little paths around the city. But it was also a city of culture, of a storied history that went back over a century, and of some of the best cuisine and sights in the entire world. It was that Manhattan that drew a young Cordelia to finish her college degree there; it was that Manhattan that she chose to start her career in, and it was that Manhattan where she first met him.

Calem.

The only name that mattered.

Calem Walters.

Her hero.

She'd see him soon enough, but for right now she was going to enjoy her own personally prescribed brand of therapy: a nice walk on a cool Manhattan summer day. It was just what the doctor ordered.

EPILOGUE

A Year Later

Cordelia had never been to a retirement party before, but the department had gone all out to send off their favorite son into civilian life. The catering hall was a beautiful place, and all around there were photos on boards from Calem's long career on the force. It was funny to see so many shots of him in a uniform, looking hardly older than a high school senior when he joined. She'd also never been in a room with so many cops wearing so much blue. It was touching to see how much love and support Calem inspired in his friends on the force.

Had it been a year already? Only twelve months ago he made the declaration, but Cordelia had only half believed that he'd follow through with it. A year was a long time, after all, and she thought he'd for sure catch another crazy case, and once that happened his sense of responsibility would take over. But he had been a man of his word, putting in all the paperwork months ahead of time to force himself to commit. He had also been a man of his word about Cordelia. He knew that neglecting her like he had neglected his past relationships would lead only one place, and he wasn't about to let her go.

Their relationship had been a storybook. Of course they had normal fights and conflicts, it wasn't perfect, but it was the type of love and compatibility that each had only seen in the movies. They balanced each other out while still being strong individuals. She knew that she wanted to be with him no matter what, and she looked forward to helping him transition to a new part of his life.

"Do you believe this?" said a voice from over her shoulder. She hadn't see Jesse as much as she would have liked; he was busy recovering and working a lot, so it didn't leave as much time for socializing as either of them would have liked. "I spent the last few weeks expecting him to rip up that paperwork and tell everyone he was playing a practical joke. Turns out I was wrong."

She gave him a big hug and looked him up and down when he let go. "You look good, Jess. You doing all right?"

"Yeah, physically I'm great. Doing all the rehab, and I finally weened myself off the pain meds. I'd say I'm at ninety-five percent."

"And what about not-physically?"

"I don't think this is the setting to have another one of our sessions, but I'm doing all right in that department too. About seventy percent."

"That's like a D in school."

"Ah, I'd call it a C minus, but what do I know, school was never my thing."

"Listen, you're right, this isn't the place for it, but if you ever want to get that up to an A plus, I know a good doctor."

"Understood. I might have to take the train, though, I'm being transferred."

"Transferred? Where? Don't tell me they gave you some boring desk job?"

"The complete opposite, actually." He sounded both disappointed and excited at the same time when he spoke. It looked like they were all transitioning into a new phase of their lives. "Queens gang unit," he said.

"Jesus, that sounds really . . ."

"Really fucking dangerous, I know." When Cordelia started to say it, she did so with some major hesitation in her voice, like a mom telling her kid not to go skydiving; but when Jesse said it he sounded like he couldn't wait for the adrenaline rush of it all. "I'm sure we'll be talking more soon, but right now I have to go shake some hands and all that bullshit."

"I understand. See you later, Jesse."

"Later."

It was good to see him, but deep down Cordelia was worried about him. He wanted to be the guy who rushes in and saves everyone so badly, and when the chance came to him he didn't get to follow through. She could tell him all day how his sacrifice had bought the time necessary for them to all survive, but that truth never really penetrated. Hopefully he'd come see her soon.

Calem was all over the room, looking handsome as ever and talking it up with all the cops in the room. He looked happy; content; satisfied with the choices he had made, and it was great for her to see him around his people for one last hurrah. He warned her that he wouldn't get to spend much time talking with her, which she understood completely, so she just walked around, having some food and looking at old pictures of Calem and a bunch of guys she didn't know.

A few hours passed like that, and then it was time for speeches. Calem's old partner from his days as a patrol cop said some heartfelt words; so did Jesse, and so did a seemingly endless parade of NYPD cops. It was all very touching to hear how much he had impacted their lives and careers. And then it was time for Calem. All the guys in the room started chanting "speech, speech, speech" at the top of their lungs until he had no choice but to reluctantly get up and take the mic. He looked amazing in his suit, and when he stood up over Cordelia he seemed like a giant.

"Do you all really need me to say something? Haven't you heard enough of me over the years?" The whole room erupted in a cacophony of laughter. "All right, fine, here it goes. Now you think I'd prepare a speech for this, knowing that I'd most likely have to stand up here and say things I don't want to say, but nope, you'd be wrong. This is all freestyle, so I apologize in advance if I say anything stupid. Get your phones ready for YouTube." He paused for a moment, lost in thought and very serious. After a minute he raised the mic back to his mouth. "Being able to serve with most of the people in this room over the years has been the honor of my life so far. We've done things together that no one will ever understand except those of us who do the job, and that's just the truth of the matter. I've gotten a lot of press and notoriety over the years for the cases I've work—all of it unwanted— but the real heroes are in this room with me tonight. You walk the streets to keep them safe, you patrol the neighborhoods, and you put your bodies on the line every day with little thanks. So, let's not make this about me, let's make it about the brave men and women who will continue to serve the city after I'm long gone. Cheers."

If the room erupted at his joke, it was like an explosion of sound when he finished that speech. Cheers of "Calem," laughter, and glasses being raised to the ceiling were everywhere, and Cordelia was overwhelmed at the love this man could generate in a room like this. It must have been a full two minutes before the noise died down enough to hear yourself think, and when it did he raised the mic to his lips once more. "I've done a lot of things over the course of my career that I'm proud of. The last two years in particular, and none of it would have been possible without the help of this woman." He was pointing to Cordelia, who had no idea she was going to part of his speech. "As many of you know she's been an invaluable tool in helping me close some of the toughest cases of the last few years. But more than that, she's helped me and my partner keep our heads on straight when we most needed it. Our minds are our greatest tools as cops, and without her I wouldn't have been able to achieve what I have these last few cases."

The room started cheering for Cordelia, which she was pretty mortified by, so she smiled awkwardly and just waved to the room of strangers, feeling both proud of his words and terribly embarrassed at the same time. He lifted the mic one last time, as Cordelia clenched as hard as she could in anticipation. "I've been a cop most of my life, and I'm going to be a civilian for the first time in twenty years. I don't know what the future is going to bring me, exactly, but I know that there's one thing that has to happen."

He put the mic down on the table and reached into his inside jacket pocket. Cordelia didn't know what he was doing, but as soon as he pulled that little black box out into the open she realized what was happening. He dropped to a single knee, and opened up the box. To her, and only to her, he asked, "Cordelia Summers, will you be my wife?" The tears were uncontrollable, and the happiness was overwhelming.

"Yes, of course I will!" she yelled, and before they were even in a full embrace the room was near deafening, with cheers and chants of "It's about time" echoing through the catering hall. It was the happiest that either of them had ever been, and it was coming at the perfect time. They kissed their first kiss as an engaged couple, and in a room of two hundred people they felt perfectly alone and content. She was going to be Cordelia Walters, and she couldn't have been more excited.

The next hour saw cake, some more drinks, and an endless parade of people congratulating them on everything. Cordelia tried to soak it all in, but it was like she was in a dream. Calem leaned over and whispered in her ear,

"I can't wait for this to be over so we can go home."

"Me too," she said. "But enjoy this. We have the rest of our lives. This celebration only lasts one night."

"I'll try," he agreed. "So, does this mean you have to come to Jiu-Jitsu with me now?"

"It absolutely doesn't, but nice try. And thanks for all the praise about helping you with the job. And by the way, I like praise as much as you do."

"I know, but I meant it. And I think you just became the official shrink for the NYPD."

"Yeah." She laughed. "I guess I should clear my calendar."

COMING SOON

Coming this November (2017) - *Jesse:* book 2 in the New York's Finest Series.

Enjoy this excerpt from the first two chapters of Jesse:

Jesse

What the fuck am I doing in Queens?

Oh yeah, I asked for this, didn't I? Typical me, looking for adventure all the time. They used to call me a cowboy when I worked homicide - *Jesse James*. God I hated that nickname, but it reminds me of how reputations can follow you wherever you go, no matter how true or false they actually are. I get where it came from I guess; I was always the first cop to raise my hand for the toughest assignment in the worst areas, even when other guys were running towards the safest situation they could find. Not me. Never me. My whole life I sought out a challenge. I never wanted anything easy because easy things are for everyone; challenges are for the few willing to meet them. And when you're surrounded by people who want to play it safe, running towards difficulty will get you labeled a cowboy. But don't believe everything you hear, I'm not a cowboy, I'm just a cop looking to do the job right.

Even now, I'm not the guy who sits behind a desk or just looks to collect a paycheck while calling myself a hero. Fuck that label. I'm the guy who runs towards the worst the city has to offer because, why else become a cop? It frankly never made sense to me to play it safe in any aspect of my life, let alone a job whose mission it is to serve and protect the people. But it's never been about danger for its own sake, I'm not really Jesse James; it's about having the most impact on people's lives. Do I need to be ticketing cars, or collaring sixteen year old turnstile jumpers in the subway? I could do that, sure, but who would I be helping? Who would I be serving? That's not to say those cops aren't necessary - they are - but that's not what I put on the blue uniform all those years ago to do.

I work in danger because danger gives the greatest opportunity to save people. And that's what this job is about - protecting people from the things they can't protect themselves from. That's what a cop is; that's why I took the job; and that's why I find myself in Queens County, New York, staking out this gang. After Calem retired I was through working homicide. I had made my mark doing that work, and honestly I'd never be as good as Calem was, even though I as his partner for a few years. For me, the real action is in the cancer of these fuckin' gangs, and that's where I can do the most good. At least I hope so. So here I am, transferred by my own request to the investigation branch of the NYPD gang unit. It's been a few months and already I hate these pieces of shit; they're an absolute plague on the city and its citizens, and my chance to make a difference here means everything to me.

If there's one thing I've learned on my short time on this job, it's that gangs transcend race, gender, and nationality. Every faction is represented on these streets: Bloods, Crips, Gangster Disciples, MS-13, the Latin Kings, The Aryan Nation, you name it. It doesn't matter if you're black, white, Hispanic, male, or female, if you live in a poor neighborhood and you're young, with no other options in life, these fuckers will scoop you up right away. They promise these young, stupid kids the world: cars, money, girls, everything - all at the tip of their fingertips, or so they tell them. All they have to do in exchange is make a deal with the devil. Beat someone; extort a local business owner; murder whoever you have to murder, it doesn't matter because the gang comes before the individual. You do what's best for your crew, no matter what. If that means you need to hurt someone, so be it; if it means you have to give up the rest of your life as a ward of the state at eighteen; so be it. The gang comes first, and in exchange they'll 'take care' of you and yours. That's the propaganda they feed these young kids, most of them ignorant, poor, and with no other hope in life.

I've seen it happen too many times in only six months on this assignment, and it breaks my heart. But the truth is that once they start flashing those signs, getting those tattoos, and picking up a life of crime instead of picking up their school books, they become my problem, and sure as hell become theirs. I don't care if they're sixteen, twenty six, or my age; if they terrorize innocent civilians they and commit crimes in my neighborhood, they're mine. I appreciate where they come from, and the sob stories really are sad to hear, but once they cross that line the time for understanding ends, and the criminal justice system steps in.

I've seen this kind of recruitment before, and even thought the time and place are completely different than where I am now, the whole situation unfolds in a shockingly similar way. I volunteered to go to Afghanistan in 2005, when I was eighteen years old. I wasn't part of the first wave of volunteers after 9/11 happened, mostly because I was too young to sign up. If I could have, I would have dropped out of high school and gone to basic training to go fuck up those guys who attacked us, but that wasn't in the cards for me. I had to wait a few years, but I got there eventually.

When I eventually got there I saw what a shit-show it was in that part of the world. Don't get me wrong, Afghanistan was a beautiful country that was mostly filled with good people just trying to live their lives, like everyone else. But I saw the Taliban operate firsthand. Not only were they complete pieces of shit who bastardized their religion in the name of terrorism, but I saw them recruit local kids, promising them glory in the afterlife if only they were willing to kill the 'infidels' Young kids; younger than these high school kids I have my eyes on now, were seduced by that bullshit story, and most of them ended up seeing the business end of an American bullet. Now I see the same thing going on right here, in my hometown of New York. Only I can do something about this.

Like I said, there's no one gang in this area. There are a whole slew of gangs, each vying for a different piece of the pie. If you ask one of these scumbags they'll tell you that they don't hurt innocent people, that the only violence they perpetrate is against other gang members, and if someone gets killed in the crossfire, then, oh well. But that's bullshit. These gangs feed off the local population like a parasite feasting on blood. They need innocent people to pay them off, to take out their aggression on, to buy their drugs, and to wash their dirty money. That's where me and my guys come in. A lot of people don't know this, but it's not against the law to be a gang member. Technically, membership doesn't constitute a crime. We have to wait until the known members commit a crime for the gang, and then we can start to put a case together, and that's where it becomes a game of cat and mouse; a game I'm playing right now.

"Who the fuck is that kid?" If it's possible, my new partner is even more of a cowboy that I was when I started with Calem back in homicide. I don't know, maybe I have a chip on my shoulder, or maybe I still feel like I have something to prove about the good I can do in this world. My partner, on the other hand, he's just a bit of a wild man who doesn't know any better yet. Ironically I'm the one trying to keep him grounded.

"Reid, chill out, he's not the important one. Focus on that other kid. The tall one who looks to be about twenty or so."

"Maybe it would help me if we used actual names, and didn't call them all 'kid'"

"I'd call them by names if we knew all of their names, relax, man, we're getting there, be patient. They're not just gonna give us what we want, we have to work for it, it's a game." Reid's not going to relax, and he's not going to be patient; it's not in his nature at all, but at least I've said my piece. He's a young cop, younger than me, full of piss and vinegar.

The kid I'm talking about- damn, I used that word again - the one I was just referring to, is wanted in more major crimes than years he's been alive. He's up there in the gang hierarchy, for sure, and for someone so young that means he's done some wicked shit on their behalf. It's my job to stop him before he hurts more people. The first thing I need to do is learn his name, and that means I need a CI.

I feel my phone vibrate three times in a row. Jesus, it's Gabby again. She's the girl I've been seeing on and off for the last month. I hate to say it, but she texts me way too much. I've asked her a bunch of times to not bother me when I'm at work unless it's an absolute emergency, but she keeps blowing up my phone for the dumbest shit. I was in the middle of a stakeout the other day when she texted to ask if I wanted to get Chinese food, then got mad when I made an issue of it. You're so mean, she said when I saw her later, I just wanted to know if you wanted Chinese, what's the big deal? I don't know if it's gonna last, to be honest, but I can't break up with the girl for texting me too much. Plus she's hot as fuck. I know how shallow that sounds, but it's the truth, the girl is an absolute smoke show - a 10/10 in the look department. Regardless of how annoying she can be, or how incompatible our lives probably are, it's hard to just walk away from a girl that hot.

The truth is I've been trying to keep my job from taking up my entire life, but it's hard. It's hard enough for cops in general, and it was really hard when I was in homicide with Calem. There were some long nights spent agonizing over evidence, and a schedule like that rarely left time for much of a personal life. Leave it to Calem to make a liar out of me on that score. Maybe I'm just making excuses, and I really can't commit to a serious relationship. Calem found a way. He was the ultimate exception to all the stereotypical cop shit: he was an intellectual, he appreciated input from others, he was only in it to help others, and he managed to sweep up the most beautiful psychologist in the city as his future wife. Why can't I find a woman as perfect for me as Cordelia is for Calem? I thought I had, but after I healed from my wounds I didn't see much of Haddie. Oh well.

But that stuff is my past. A recent past, sure, but when you do what I do, every day brings new adventures, and that stuff with Haddie feels like an eternity ago. Like I said, oh well. Right now I have to focus on this situation that's happening in front of me. I. . . I mean we - we need to figure out who's doing what, and that's gonna take all of my attention. I need to keep these streets as safe as I can. Now, back to this guy across the street.

What that fuck is that kid's name?

Haddie

Okay, I admit it, I have issues.

Nothing surprising there, I know, but I really think it's time to admit it to myself. You have issues, Haddie, time to work on yourself! I guess that word makes me sound crazy, but in reality I just need to get my life back in order. Ever since I moved here from California last year life has been as crazy and disorganized. What started as a short stay with my good friend Cordelia turned into an extended vacation where I let myself forget adult things like paying bills and working for a living. And to top it all off, in the middle of what was supposed to be a week-long trip back home to the Big Apple I was almost the victim of a horrific crime by The Manhattan Rapist - a guy named Johnathan Kenenna who was in the midst of terrorizing the women of the city. I got off easy compared to the Jesse and Cordelia - just a few bruises and scars - and all of us got off easy compared to the women who were his actual victims. But still, it was a crazy thing to have happen.

It took a while to get over that whole ordeal - if that's even the kind of thing you can get over, and another few weeks of helping Jesse rehab after he took a bullet trying to save Cordelia and I. He went through a special kind of hell in trying to get better after taking a slug to the stomach, and I tried to be there for him as a friend as much as I could. Friend. I guess we were more like acquaintances who were on

162

the road to something more - maybe - but he literally got shot while coming to pick me up on our first date, and after that I was more like his nurse than anything else. I honestly don't know why nothing every started up between us again after he got better, but sometimes people just drift apart. It's not like we were close, just acquaintances like I said, and he stayed in the city for another year after he recovered as I moved out to Queens.

Queens, the borough I'm currently calling home.

It had been Cordelia's idea when I told her that I was thinking of staying in New York full time, and she was right about places to live being much cheaper here than in the City. Don't get me wrong, there are ridiculous places in Queens where the property values are some of the most expensive in the area, but there are also have more affordable housing than the heart of Manhattan. So here I am, a Queens girl, trying to get her life back in order after a crazy few months. The best part about being back has been Cordelia. Having a good friend around to help me land on my feet and get reintegrated into being a New Yorker has made the transition that much easier.

Even so, there are still things that being a California girl for the last few years has made difficult when it comes to getting back into New York mode. The differences between the two places are stark in some ways. New York really is a much faster place, and no one is ever that relaxed. It's part of what makes the city amazing, but it also takes some getting used to after you've been out of it for a while, surfing and taking in the sun on the beaches of L.A. But I'm back now, and I'm already starting to feel my inner New Yorker coming out to play. And I'm going to start my day with a standard New York thing - an egg bagel with cream cheese. I missed the bagels and pizza when I was in California. There's nothing quite like a New York bagel, or a New York bagel shop, for that matter. I have a good one near me.

I moved into a little apartment in Flushing, a diverse neighborhood with a lot of immigrant families from different parts of the world that's only a short distance from Manhattan. When I was a kid Flushing was different, but the influx of people from different parts of Asia and Latin America has made it a really interesting place to live. And the food! It's hard to walk around any part of the neighborhood without having your mouth practically water. There's food from Columbia, Italy, China - basically every type of cuisine that you could ever want, all concentrated in a small part of a large borough of New York. It's a cooler place to live than I would have thought when I was living in Manhattan.

So, like I said, now I'm a Queens girl, and this particular Queens girl needs a job! I've been living off savings I had from selling my photography studio, but the well is starting to run dry and I need to stop being lazy and get a real job. Luckily Cordelia was nice enough to hook me up with a friend of hers who runs a center for at-risk youth not far from me. I'm on my way there now. I've never worked with kids before, let alone teens, and let alone teens with issues, but I think I might actually have a knack for it. What most people don't know is that I was one of those kids myself. You wouldn't know it after seeing that I went to an Ivy League school, but I almost got expelled from high school in the 9th grade. I was a troubled kid from a troubled home, and if it wasn't for the intervention of the right guidance counselor I would have been just another statistic of a kid lost to the streets.

That seems like such a long time ago; a Haddie who doesn't even exist anymore. I'd love to be able to live off my bank account forever, but that's not realistic. If I have to have a job I'd like to have one that feels like I'm giving something back to the community, or just making a difference in a kid's life. I think I'd be good at that because I've been there. Hopefully they're good kids even if they get in trouble all the time.

I text Cordelia to thank her one more time, and in no time at all I get a text back that reads "You'll do great, and Jennifer is the best, just be yourself and you'll be fine!" She's always super positive like that, and it was great of her to hook me up like this. I know the job won't pay much, but then again I'm a low-maintenance chick - even the place I'm renting is practically for nothing, so anything they pay me is fine. Plus I still have some money left from my business, so I'll be alright. We're finally here, and the best part is knowing I get to remove myself from this sweatbox of gross guys rubbing themselves up against me.

This part of flushing isn't the nicest, but I guess you don't open a place like this in a nice neighborhood. What's that funny name? NIMBY! Not in my backyard. That's what happens with things like a home for troubled youth, or prisons, or low-budget housing; everyone thinks they're a great idea but no one wants it near them. So it ends up that the places where people need the most help are usually in the worst areas. Ironic. But I'm comfortable almost anywhere. Like I said, I'm a really low maintenance chick.

I walk a block from the bus station and the area doesn't get any nicer the further I walk. Minus the prison they have all of things I just described. There are tall, low income housing apartments everywhere, and public parks that look like they haven't been updated in years. In the distance, on the corner of a block next to a bunch of cheap stores is the place. The dilapidated sign on the outside reads "Teen Shelter", which is nondescript enough to not really describe what the place is. The word 'shelter' makes me think all sorts of things before I even walk in the door: homeless people, criminals just released from prison - basically nothing good, but I don't want to walk in with a bad attitude. It's the first word that's more important than the second.

Kids. They're still just kids. . .

To be continued in November. . .

FOLLOW CHRISTOPHER

To keep up with the latest releases in the New York's Finest series, follow me on all my social media.

My Website
www.authorchristopherharlan.com

Twitter
@chris_harlan35

Email:
Christopherharlan35@gmail.com

My Facebook Reader's Group (Harlan's Readers)

ACKNOWLEDGMENTS

First and foremost, I have my family to thank for their support through all of these books. Without that there would be no words to write.

Secondly, I thank everyone who reads these words - my readers who purchased the book, read on KU, or read an ARC for me - you make this all possible with the time you spend with these books, and I never take that for granted.

Thirdly, I have to thank those who most directly helped this book become what it is. To my cover designer and formatter, Jessica Hildreth, you've been a godsend to work with - efficient, available, affordable, and of the highest quality. To Marla, my copy editor, for catching all those mistakes, thank you for working quickly on my behalf.

A few special thanks are also in order:

To BT Urruela, for asking me to join the Romance & Erotica (R&E) fraternity, and allowing me a much wider audience for my work than I ever imagined, and for being accessible and just plain cool.

To all those in the frat with me: BT Urruela (once again), Derek Adam, Golden Czermak, Seth Nicholas King, Mickey Miller, and Scott Hildreth - you've been nothing but kind, available, and helpful whenever I needed help, and you're all amazing authors. I hope everyone reading this gets all of their books as well, you won't be disappointed.

To Scott Hildreth, who gave freely of his time to engage in a simple conversation that impacted me more than it must have seemed on the other end of the line. Sometimes it's the small moments in life that can propel you forward into something larger. .. stay tuned.

And finally to Lauren Lascola-Lesczynski, not only for the tireless amounts of work she puts in to the R&E fraternity for all of us, but also for helping organize this release. For your help as a beta-reader, for helping arrange the release party, for organizing my ARC team, and a million other micro-tasks, you have my eternal thanks. This truly would've been infinitely harder without your selfless assistance. Let's keep it rolling. . .

ALSO BY CHRISTOPHER HARLAN – THE IMPRESSIONS SERIES (BOOKS 1 & 2)

Impressions of You

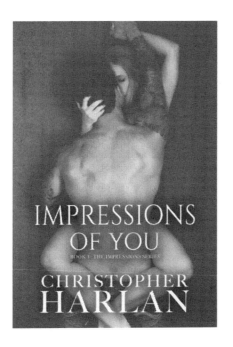

Wesley Marsden is the heir to the successful company, Marsden, Inc. From the outside he seems to have it all: wealth, good looks, and a genius level IQ, but these qualities hide the depths of his complexity. While he's a man who's strong, confident, and in control, he's also a man obsessed with solving a family mystery that has left him with a sometimes crippling case of social anxiety, and plagued his personal relationships for years.

Mia Careri is a stunningly beautiful special needs elementary teacher; a woman who's devoted her life to the care and education of other people's children. Funny, beautiful, and intelligent, she has a job she loves and close friends who are like her family. The only elusive aspect of her life has been finding a man who understands who she is at her core, and appreciates the sacrifices she makes on a daily basis. Plagued by insecurities and a slew of failed relationships, she yearns for the missing facet of her life so far—the perfect man to have a future with.

Soon both of their fates will collide over the course of a fateful few months, and neither of them will ever be the same again.

Impressions of Me

We can try to deny our deepest desires, but we can never truly erase them from our hearts.

I've always wanted something more from life, and until I saw him again that fateful afternoon I had pretty much given up on things getting better. I didn't know exactly what I was missing until I saw Kane again, and it only took one look into his eyes to reawaken the feeling I had the first time I laid eyes on him. We met under such strange and dramatic circumstances over a year ago, when I was just the supportive best friend who tagged along to his house, and he was just Wesley's worried little brother. I knew that some part of me wanted him even then, and what I thought would be something between us fell apart before it ever really began.

Now he's come back into my life as unexpectedly as he left it. That life's been a mess lately—I'm stuck in a dead-end job that I hate, I have a best friend who's married and moved away, and now a dark cloud from my past looms in the distance, threatening to destroy everything that I love. I don't know what the future will bring between me and Kane, but I know that I want him, and that he may turn out to be my redemption.

PRAISE FOR IMPRESSIONS OF YOU

"Christopher Harlan didn't just step in the literary world; he busted the damn door down. He knows how to write a story that will keep you engaged... His characters are well thought out with a depth that surprised me. The romance is beautiful, heartwarming and poignant."
-Amanda, <u>Tears & Lipstick Smears Book Blog</u>

"Impressions of You, starring Mia Careri and Wesley Marsden, is the love story not only of these two characters, but also of a man's deep love for his family...this is a great story and I can't wait to see what the author does with the extra characters. Great things will come from this author, I have no doubt!"
-Corrie, <u>Goodreads.com reader</u>

"Impressions of You is a debut book by Christopher Harlan that simply told a beautiful story of love, pain and letting go. It was a memorable and a beautiful written story that I simply could not get enough of. I enjoyed reading it immensely... I did not expect at all the situations in this book to be so profound but I was left with a sense of contentment

while I was reading this story. Christopher Harlan wrote a book that had real issues which made it so captivating to me. In a way, it gave the story such a different edge."
-Tanaka, <u>The Romantic Angel Blog</u>

"This book will make you see the highs and lows, and it will turn you inside out and then right you. I loved this read and am seriously looking forward to more from this Author.
Get writing Mr. Harlan."
-Julie, <u>Goodreads.com reader</u>

AMAZON REVIEWS OF IMPRESSIONS OF YOU

"...Not only is he super interactive with his readers he is also attentive and caring... He kept in touch with me at all times to check if I had any concerns in regards to what I was reading... To me that speaks wonders of an author...
I definitely recommend Impressions of You to any reader willing to give a male author a chance in this romance genre... I will be placing Christopher Harlan in my list of authors to follow... Thank you for an amazing read!!"
- Dianela's Details

"...Everything about this book, from the HOT and incredibly sexy cover to the captivating and engaging storyline was pure perfection and I am so happy that I decided to purchase this book and give it a chance. A rare gem in the Indie world of books, Christopher Harlan has knocked it out of the park with Impressions of You and I can't wait for the second installment from this incredible author."
-Tamara B.

Made in the USA
Columbia, SC
24 February 2018